CAILLOU PETTIS

While You Sleep

First published by Falcon Publishing 2022

Copyright © 2022 by Caillou Pettis

All rights reserved. No part of this publication may be reproduced, stored or transmitted in any form or by any means, electronic, mechanical, photocopying, recording, scanning, or otherwise without written permission from the publisher. It is illegal to copy this book, post it to a website, or distribute it by any other means without permission.

This novel is entirely a work of fiction. The names, characters and incidents portrayed in it are the work of the author's imagination. Any resemblance to actual persons, living or dead, events or localities is entirely coincidental.

Caillou Pettis asserts the moral right to be identified as the author of this work.

Content Warning: This collection features a number of scenes, scenarios, and descriptions that could potentially cause emotional distress.

First edition

Cover art by Donnie Goodman

*This book was professionally typeset on Reedsy.
Find out more at reedsy.com*

Contents

WHILE YOU SLEEP	1
PRAISE FOR CAILLOU PETTIS	2
DEDICATION	3
WHILE YOU SLEEP	4
BIRTHDAY BUMPS	13
HE'LL BE BACK	24
THE FACE	31
THE ANTIQUE STORE	38
103.9 NEWRYST FM	86
HIVES	95
LAST SHIFT	103
WEBS	115
WHERE AM I?	122
STORY NOTES	127
ACKNOWLEDGEMENTS	140
ABOUT THE AUTHOR	146

WHILE YOU SLEEP

Stories by
Caillou Pettis

PRAISE FOR CAILLOU PETTIS

"An anthology meticulously curated by Pettis, WHILE YOU SLEEP is a genuinely disturbing assortment of tales. With no shortage of blood, nightmares, and haunted objects, Newryst is one place you won't be leaving alive. At least not with your sanity intact..."

-Patrick Delaney, author of *The House That Fell From The Sky*

"Pettis's *WHILE YOU SLEEP* is a horror collection with bite. For anyone who has ever been tempted to sleep with the lights on, these stories are sure to get under your skin in the most delicious way. Don't miss this one."

-Briana Morgan, author of *The Tricker-Treater and Other Stories*

DEDICATION

*For Korynn. Thank you for always being my number one supporter.
I love you to the moon and to Saturn.*

WHILE YOU SLEEP

Do you ever stop and wonder exactly what happens while you sleep? Sure, we as humans understand that, while we sleep, we don't have any full recollection of what exactly happens because, after all, that's the whole point of sleep. Sleeping is an everyday regimen that allows our bodies to shut down for about eight hours in order for our brain to be refueled and ready for the next day to come.

Dreams can obviously occur while we are sleeping, but what about the real world? When we sleep, what goes on in the world around us? Do you ever worry that you are being watched by an unwanted visitor? Maybe somebody has managed to creep into your house and they are now hiding in your closet, peeking at you while you lay in bed completely oblivious.

So, I ask again - do you ever worry that you are being watched by an unwanted visitor? If not...

You should be.

This is exactly what happened to a thirty-year-old man named Everett Campbell. Everett had an ordinary job working as a retail manager at a local clothing store that paid a decent yearly salary. He had a couple of friends from work that he enjoyed spending some time with on the weekends and lived in a nice, spacious home in his hometown of Newryst.

But things could be more than a little lonely for Everett most of the time, mainly because he didn't have a lady friend to keep him company. Everett had tried dating many times but he always managed to screw things up. Sometimes he was unable to commit fully to the relationship or other times, he found that he and his new love interest were looking for two completely different things.

Everett felt like a loser because all of his friends who were his age either had girlfriends of five years or wives. And yet here he was with absolutely nobody to go home to. But it's okay because at least he has one visitor to keep him company.

Albeit, one that Everett does not wish to be around.

Ever since he was a young boy, Everett has had problems sleeping properly. No matter how long he lays in his bed, he simply cannot manage to fall asleep without taking some sort of a sleeping pill. Of course, when he was a lot younger, his dad would always blame it on him watching too much television.

"Well, maybe if you would turn off that god-damned TV once in a while, your brain wouldn't be so malformed!", Mr. Campbell would yell. But even as a kid, Everett knew that was just a bunch of bullshit. All of his friends from school watched television just as much as he did and yet they all managed to get to bed on time and had eight full hours of rest every night.

Everett was overweight ever since the age of thirteen. Even back then, he weighed 250 lbs and always did his best to exercise and get in shape, but it often failed after he promised to eat just *one* donut, but it eventually turned into a full dozen. In his thirties, Everett weighs a total of 318 lbs. Despite wanting to lose weight and better his health, the thing he wanted to do more than anything else was to fix his sleep problems.

At night, Everett would turn on the television in his room, watching some dumb soap opera he didn't know the name of, hoping it would act as some sort of a faux sleeping pill for him but it never worked. Did he find the show boring? Absolutely. But even watching the overly dramatic lives of some twenty-something couple was not enough to make him snooze off. Even still, he decided he had better turn the television off to save some electricity money.

As he stared off into seemingly nowhere specific, Everett thought *I'm never gonna fucking fall asleep. I'm just gonna sit here with my eyes wide open all night* even though he didn't want that at all. He had hoped that perhaps his brain would eventually grow tired of being awake and would simply force Everett to *get the fuck to sleep* but he knew that was wishful thinking.

Or was it?

Everett lay in his bed completely silent with his eyes shut, but he knew that somehow, somewhere throughout the course of the night, he had done the impossible. He had fallen asleep, and he didn't feel quite so tired at the moment. He had wanted to leap out of bed and kiss the floor. He wanted to thank the Heavens that God had finally done him a favor and allowed him to *get some fucking sleep*.

The only problem was that Everett could not move. Literally. Upon opening his eyes, and rubbing the sleep from the corners of his pupils, he had felt an extreme twinge of absolute terror course through his neck, eyes, heart, stomach, legs, and arms.

He was staring directly at a demon.

But this wasn't just any old demon. It certainly wasn't one that he would expect to see when entering the gates of Hell. This demon was different than anything anybody could ever imagine. The entity was almost entirely dark with piercing white eyes, long limber arms and legs, and red cracks in its skin.

Not only was the demon absolutely terrifying to look at, but it was quite literally crushing Everett's windpipe by being perched on his chest, its clawed, pointy legs digging deep into the poor man's chest.

But no matter how much pain, shock, and awe Everett was in, he couldn't scream. He had tried with all his might, and yet not a single sound would come out of his mouth. Not even a little whimper could creep out of his throat. To make matters worse, his body was rendered totally immobile.

Even though the demon was not pinning down Everett's arms or legs, he found that he couldn't move even a single finger muscle. The only thing in the world that Everett was capable of doing at that moment was staring directly into the fierce white eyes of the creature, its claws, and legs digging deep into his skin.

He felt more pain at that moment than he had ever felt before in his entire life. More than anything else in the world, he wanted to scream *SOMEONE HELP ME! SOMEONE GET THIS FUCKING THING OFF OF ME! HELP! HELP!*

But his mouth wouldn't even move. His arms, legs, toes, and fingers might as well have been severed off because he couldn't use them either way. As Everett stared deep into the eyes of the demon perching atop his chest, he had a strange thought.

Does this thing know that I'm scared of it? He didn't really think it mattered, anyway. He was confident that this demon wanted Everett to be absolutely horrified, but even if he wasn't scared one bit (which he was), the demon wouldn't simply let him go. Everett was now his prisoner. As for how long, that was anybody's guess.

The only thing Everett knew was that he was probably going to die any moment now. He swore he could feel his entire soul drain from his body with each passing second the demon stayed atop his body.

What was strange to Everett, as well, was that this demon didn't have any sort of facial expression while this was happening. Everett had already taken notice of the creature's burning white eyes and its mouth, but never once did it open wide to show a large set of grizzled, pointy teeth. It simply sat on top of the man's chest, both parties locking eyes with each other as if taking part in some sick and twisted staring contest.

Although Everett could not even move his head left or right, he could ever-so-slightly make out things in his room out of his peripheral vision. His window curtains had been pulled aside, allowing for him to get a view of the city outside.

Everything outside was still shrouded in darkness, and Everett wondered what everybody else was doing at this time of the night. Whatever it was the rest of the citizens of this once peaceful city were doing, he was willing to bet that nobody was going through the same thing he was at this moment.

A couple of minutes had gone by since awakening, and Everett was shocked to find that no matter how much pain and suffering he was in, he was not dead yet. He was confident that he would've died by now because of just how much soul-crushing agony he was in.

But here he was, still looking into the face of his tormentor, and the tormentor looking right back at him as if he or rather *it*, was doing absolutely nothing wrong. Was this just part of this demon's life? Did this demon not know anything to do other than perch on Everett's chest?

And how in the world had he even gotten into Everett's bedroom in the first place? It was a thought that coursed all throughout the man's mind and yet no matter how deeply he thought about it, he could not come up with a logical explanation.

He figured that if this was indeed a demon, it didn't really need a logical entryway to get inside. After all, it *is* a *demon*. The laws of the real world don't necessarily apply to these types of entities. The world is their oyster, and they'll do whatever the hell they want inside of it.

All of a sudden, Everett started to feel the entire world around him vibrate. He felt his brain matter getting sucked down his body. It wasn't painful per se, but it was a feeling that Everett knew he definitely did not like experiencing.

While this was happening, Everett noticed the entire room was being engulfed by an ever-growing red light, soaking up the entire room. And rather than finally getting off of Everett's chest, the demon proceeded to grow about six feet taller than it already was.

It proceeded to outstretch its long, gangling arms toward Everett's neck where it made a strike, causing a trickle of blood to go splatter against the walls, but miraculously, Everett was still alive.

He found that was also able to close his eyes for ten seconds before they involuntarily opened once again. The room was still cloaked in an all-encompassing red light that devoured everything else in the room.

But much to Everett's pleasure, his tormentor was nowhere to be found. He was no longer on his chest, and he felt like he could finally breathe as best as he could, despite having a massive, gaping portion of his neck sliced open.

Even though the demon was nowhere to be seen, Everett found that he was still unable to move any part of his body. His eyes were unblinking, his arms and legs were rendered totally useless. He had no idea what he should be doing. He tried to scream once again, but his mouth wouldn't even form the words that he wanted so desperately to fly out.

Then, he felt it again. The soul-sucking sensation. He felt as if his life was just about to end, and he didn't know how it was possible. The demon wasn't even there.

Out of nowhere, the room all around Everett was set ablaze, with all of the objects in his room slowly burning and crumbling to nothing but ash and dust. The sound of fire engulfing the room around Everett was utterly terrifying as it quickly began to get closer and closer to where he lay.

He knew at this moment that this was it. There was simply no getting out of this no matter how hard he tried. Even if he was somehow able to get out of bed at that very moment, it would simply be much too late for him to try to make a daring escape out of the building.

Panic was bubbling to the surface of Everett's face. He didn't know what else to do but simply stare and watch as the world around him crumbled to nothing but fire and dust. All of a sudden, Everett heard the loudest voice he had ever heard speak directly into his ears, causing his eardrums to immediately shatter after hearing what this voice had to say.

WELCOME TO HELL!

Finally, Everett could move his body, but he was no longer in his room in the city of Newryst. He was in the last place he wanted to be. Surrounded by flames. Demons. Agony. Torture.

Everett took a look at his arms and legs and noticed that his skin had turned bright red and appeared cracked and scaly. But, now, Everett no longer felt scared or worried. He no longer felt like his whole world was gone. He felt like he was home, and a smile slowly started to form on his face. He looked up and saw the unmistakable face of the Devil himself sitting on a throne directly in front of him, surrounded by flames.

Out of all the possible questions Everett could have asked the Devil, he only asked one - one that took even the Devil by surprise.

"Is there such thing as sleep here?", he asked.

The Devil merely glanced at Everett for a few passing moments before eventually answering, "You are never going to have to sleep again. You are mine now".

Everett should have felt petrified. He was in Hell, and he was a servant of the Devil. But against all odds, he replied to the Devil with just two words - "Thank you".

BIRTHDAY BUMPS

Gavin doesn't remember anything from the past few days. The only reason he knows that he hasn't seen the outside world in that long is that he can feel extreme hunger and thirst bubbling inside of him, his body telling him to put any sort of fuel inside because it can't go on much longer.

His memory is foggy and his head feels like it's been clouded up to the point where even thinking about something as simple as the clothes he was currently wearing was too much for his brain to comprehend.

The one thing he immediately thought was more than a little strange was the room he was currently sitting inside. He knew without a shadow of a doubt that the last time he was in the outside world, it was some day in June in the year 2022, and yet, for some reason, the room he was in made him feel like he had been transported all the way back to the 1980s.

From the horrendously ugly wallpaper down to the couch he was currently strapped to, all the way to the bizarre and hideous boxy television set stationed directly in front of him on an old table, he knew that either one of two things was happening:

One: he had indeed been transported back to the 1980s and even though he had been the biggest fan of the 1980s despite being a seventeen-year-old living in a world where people stream the newest rap hits instead of the oldies, he didn't necessarily like the idea of time travel too much. He liked living in the present.

Or, two: Whoever or *whatever* brought him here was obsessed with 80s decor. That, or this person simply couldn't afford to have this room furnished with anything more modern or up-to-date.

But none of that really mattered right now. Gavin needed to get answers. He needed to find out why he was here, and most importantly, where *here* was. The room where he sit strapped to a couch had zero windows in sight. He could move his head left and right, and wasn't all that surprised to find the room had no windows.

After all, it would be quite the dumb thing to have in a room where kidnapping victims go. All they need is a little bit of strength to break the window and they'd be free once more. Gavin's kidnapper wasn't that dumb.

The thing that struck Gavin the most, though, was that there appeared to be no door anywhere throughout the room. If that was the case, then how did *he* get here in the first place?

It was then that Gavin realized there probably *was* a door in this room somewhere, albeit a secret one that blended in with the wallpaper of the room so as to make Gavin panic.

Despite all this though, Gavin wasn't all that antsy. Yes, he wanted to get out of this room as soon as possible and go home to his mom and dad who were definitely wondering where he was at the moment, but he also knew that he would find a way out. He was a resourceful kid.

After a few minutes went by, Gavin's head felt less cloudy, causing him to be more alert to the scenario he was in. It wasn't good. He didn't need a clear head to know that, though.

One of the things that shocked him the most was that he realized the only thing that was keeping him strapped down to the chair was dozens of pieces of duct tape. Whoever or *what*ever placed him on the chair didn't even have handcuffs? Was this intentional? Or was this kidnapper not as smart as Gavin initially thought?

Gavin was a strong kid, weighing 200 lbs and most of it being muscle. As early as three years ago, though, this was not the case. His parents had to convince Gavin to exercise more often and get into shape because "You never know when you're gonna need it".

Seeing as how he is a kid, Gavin doesn't always listen to everything his parents tell him, but he was certainly glad that he took their advice to exercise and get fit because he had a good feeling that he could free himself from this chair. He just needed some effort.

Thud! Thud! Gavin kicked his legs against the chair to free himself of the duct tape. Once again, he was surprised at just how easy it was to free himself from this predicament.

What kind of kidnapper goes out of their way to ensure that their victim is placed inside a room with no visible doors or windows but is unable to find strong tape to tie them down? "Alright, let's see…", Gavin pondered.

Even though there was nothing in his way of escape now, he knew that it wasn't going to be as easy as simply standing up from the couch and feeling against the wall for where the door is.

And even if by some miraculous chance that *was* how easy it would be, he didn't know where *exactly* he was. What if he opened the secret door only to find that his captor was waiting on the other side?

But, on the other hand, Gavin also knew that he couldn't be in here forever. Sometimes, you need to take a little bit of a risk if it means your freedom and life are on the line.

So, not knowing what else to do, Gavin slowly but surely rose from the chair only to find that his body was unbelievably stiff. He remembered how his dad always said things like "Man, I'm getting old. I used to be able to walk the park with no problem. But now? I can barely get down the stairs without feeling like I'm gonna fall over".

Gavin always just shook his head and thought *It's an old people thing*, but now, he realized that he could relate to what his dad was going through. His spine felt like somebody had shattered it by taking a massive sledgehammer with extreme might, breaking off every piece of bone imaginable.

His legs felt as if they had been turned to jelly. As he slowly made his best effort to stand on his feet, he realized that his entire body was wobbling. He couldn't stand upright for even one full second before collapsing right back on the couch in complete and utter defeat.

Maybe I've been drugged and the side effects are kicking in, Gavin thought or, rather, prayed. Even if he *did* make it out of here alive, he felt like he would be better off dead than live the rest of his life with this much back pain. He'd rather be drugged and feel this way for hours than actually having his back broken and him just not remembering it.

Once more, he did his best to slowly but steadily stand up, being careful so as not to pull any muscles in his body. This time, instead of feeling excruciating back and spinal pain, he felt an extreme electrical shock course through his ears, causing him to yell as loud as he could before crashing back onto the couch.

Immediately afterward, his ears began to ring shrilly for a solid minute, while Gavin writhed in discomfort on the couch. As early as two minutes ago, Gavin was confident that he was going to get out of here with no problems. Now, however, not so much.

Then, Gavin did something he realized he probably should have done first: check his pants pockets to see if his phone was there. He wasn't surprised to find that it was gone. He knew this kidnapper wasn't too bright, but he would've been laughably stupid had he allowed Gavin to keep his phone.

Although he feared for his own safety more than anything right now, Gavin also couldn't help but wonder what his friends and family were doing at the moment. Maybe Ethan was hanging out at the skate park, trying to perfect the Pop Shove-it 360 that he had been practicing every day.

His mom was probably at home watching some corny soap opera as she always did. Or, maybe she was putting on one of her vinyl records and dancing around the kitchen in the refrigerator light with her husband.

Thinking about those memories hurt, because although Gavin and his parents didn't always enjoy the same hobbies, they all three loved listening to music together. Dancing to it, singing along to the words.

Recently, Gavin had purchased *1989 (Taylor's Version)* on vinyl, one of the rare albums that absolutely everybody in his family enjoyed listening to. Their musical taste was similar but his dad could be a bit picky when it came to music. That's why whenever they all agreed upon an album being great, it was cause for celebration.

Gavin found it strange that, more than anything else, he wanted to go home and listen to a vinyl record with his parents. He didn't want anything to eat or drink despite how starved and dehydrated he was. He didn't want to go hang out with his friends at the skate park. He wanted to go home and belt "They are the hunters, we are the foxes / And we run!" at the top of his lungs with his parents.

But he knew that wasn't going to happen anytime soon. Gavin sat sprawled out on the couch in defeat when out of nowhere, the old boxy television in front of him turned on, displaying a screen of solid static for about ten seconds.

It was just a television screen, but seeing it turn on all by itself caused Gavin's stomach to feel horrible. He knew that televisions couldn't simply turn on by themselves. He realized that the only way this could have been turned on was if somebody was nearby holding a remote, but as he look around the entire room, he couldn't find a single soul in sight.

He continued to scan the room before he eventually snapped his head back toward the television screen after hearing a strikingly familiar voice. The video on the television screen was playing an old family video of Gavin as a baby boy.

Gavin had never seen this video before. If he was being shown this video at home by his parents, he probably would've been deeply interested in seeing his younger self but right now, he felt more uneasy than he did just moments ago.

Who had gotten a video of him when he was just a baby? And why were they showing this to Gavin? Was this some sort of sick and twisted surprise birthday party that his family was throwing? His birthday was in June after all; but no. Gavin knew his parents and any of his friends would never go to *these* extremes for a party.

After the video of Gavin as a baby had finished playing, another one played immediately afterward, this time it was of him on his first birthday. His parents could be heard in the kitchen singing the birthday song while Gavin sat in a baby chair looking completely and totally confused.

He didn't know what to do other than to sit there and stare at the television screen. He didn't want to yell for help or anything in case his captor would hear him. He knew that if he had to fight back he would fail miserably. After all, how can you fight somebody off when your back feels like it's been shattered in pieces?

An endless stream of videos played one after the other. Each one was filmed on Gavin's birthday, but as each video was cued up, he felt more and more uncomfortable.

But he felt the most uncomfortable as soon as he got to the video for his seventeenth birthday because that was the most recent birthday he had celebrated. He wasn't sure what was going to happen after that video was finished playing.

In the video for his seventeenth birthday, Gavin was holding a cake his parents had made for him and after they were done singing the birthday song, Gavin blew out his candles before immediately grabbing a knife and cutting a piece for himself.

Then... *static*. As soon as the video had finished playing, Gavin rapidly looked around the room for any sign of a way out. He didn't know what to do. He didn't want to try to stand up again in the fear of his back causing him more pain than ever before, so once again, he simply sat there with nothing else in the whole world left to do except for wait.

After about a solid minute of waiting, the television screen turned back on, only this time, the video that was playing was very different. It was different because on the bottom right-hand corner, the date read "June 28, 2022: 15:02". Gavin's birthday. It's today.

But what made Gavin's heart sink even more was that he realized that this video was filmed inside the very room he was sitting in. Not only that, it looked as if Gavin could see himself on the video... sitting down in an old-fashioned chair... looking at a television screen.

Immediately, Gavin snapped his head around and saw a strange figure wearing a black suit and a bunny mask staring directly at him.

"Who the fuck are you?!" Gavin shouted at the mysterious figure. "Shhh", the figure insisted, while placing his pointer finger up to his lips.

"No! Fuck this! I'm not being quiet! Where the fuck am I? Huh? Tell me where the fuck I am, right now!", Gavin screamed.

"It's okay. You're safe here. I wanted to wish you a happy birthday", the figure said. "Do you have any birthday traditions?".

"Besides opening presents, no", Gavin replied. "Well, how about I start one for you? Have you ever heard of the birthday bumps?", the figure asked.

Gavin didn't want to be talking to this unsettling character, but he realized it would be best to co-operate rather than fight. "Yes, I've heard of it and I know what it is, but I've never done it".

"In that case, why not give a try today?", the figure said with a glimmer of glee in its voice. Before Gavin even had the opportunity to move, the masked figure reached down to the floor where it proceeded to pick up a massive sledgehammer.

Gavin's eyes went wide. He knew what was coming, and he knew that if he wanted to live to see another day, he would have to miraculously have some sort of superhuman healing power that would allow for his back to be fully repaired and for his legs to be stable.

Before he even had the chance to try to stand up, the figure had made a large swing with the sledgehammer, making a direct hit on the boy's back.

"One!", the figure chanted, as Gavin fell face-first to the floor, writhing in agony. "Two!", he yelled after making another crushing blow to the boy's back. This time, bones could be audibly heard snapping in several different places.

"Three! Four! Five! Six!", the figure screamed with a sadistic hint of glee in its voice. By the time the figure swung the sledgehammer ten times, Gavin was no longer recognizable. His body was scattered around the floor in clumps of limbs and body parts.

"Eleven! Twelve!", the figure swung down the hammer right against Gavin's head, causing it to explode the same way a watermelon does when there are too many rubber bands wrapped around it. Chunks of brain matter flew across the room, leaving stains on the figure's otherwise clean suit.

"Seventeen!", the figure smashed down on the few remaining bits of Gavin's body that were left on the ground. For the eighteenth and final blow, the figure wound up more than ever before, before coming flying down with the sledgehammer, screeching "EIGHTEEN!".

Blood splattered all over the room as the masked figure grunted and exhaled rapidly, dropping the sledgehammer with a loud clatter to the floor.

The figure knelt down to the ground and proceeded to scoop up the remaining chunks of the young boy before eating them savagely. As he chewed and swallowed the last bite, the figure said "Happy birthday Gavin. I hope you made a good final wish".

HE'LL BE BACK

Do you remember just how great sleepovers used to be when you were a kid? There was simply nothing quite like the good old days of inviting your best friend over to your house or vice versa, knowing that an entire night of movies, video games, pizza, and adventures was awaiting. When I was a kid up until about the age of thirteen, I practically had sleepovers every weekend with my still lifelong best friend Nick, which usually consisted of us going to one another's house and staying up playing the newest *Merrytown Legends* installment and trying to level up our characters.

More often than not, Nick would sleepover at my house simply because there was some strange feeling I got whenever I slept over at another friends' house. The sheets would never feel right, the darkness of the house would feel all too surrounding and the sheer lack of my parents would freak me out. Even though I knew I would most likely be safe, I still had that gut feeling of dread, so Nick came over to my house to sleep over and most times, he didn't mind.

In November of 2010, ten-year-old me invited Nick to sleep over at my house to which he gladly obliged because he wanted to spend time with me and play some video games. My childhood room was always considered by all of my friends to be the smallest bedroom they'd ever been in. Basically, the only things my blue flower-print wallpapered room were able to withhold was my television, video game consoles, a closet, and a teeny bookshelf. That, and my window which looked out onto my backyard.

As soon as Nick came over for the day, we made the impromptu decision to do everything we could to pull an all-nighter which is something we almost never did. A lot of times we would stay up until about midnight or so, but we would always go to bed *eventually*. This time, however, we wanted to see if we could muster up the energy to stay up the entire night playing games. We had an agreement that if one of us felt tired to the point of falling asleep, we would go downstairs, get an energy drink and get some fresh air.

So there we were - it was about one in the morning and I was playing *Merrytown Legends* while Nick lay on my bed watching me play in a multiplayer lobby, while he started to drift off a bit. When I noticed this, I quickly shook him but for some reason, I didn't really feel like going downstairs to do our agreed plan. Instead, I simply gazed out into the cool November night sky, looking out into the horizon.

My childhood home was right beside a highway so by looking out my room's window and looking upward, you could see past the highway as cars zoomed by in the shadow of night. Curious, Nick looked outside as well just to see what captured my attention, but was disappointed and confused when he realized that I was simply looking at nothing.

At least, it was nothing for a while.

My backyard was absolutely massive - massive to the point where you could literally play a game of soccer in it and have plenty of room for at least ten players. In this backyard were two sheds and two slopes that were absolutely perfect to toboggan down in the winter. During the night of the sleepover, while looking out my window, something in my backyard suddenly caught my attention and chilled my blood cold.

Inside the shed closest to the backyard porch, I noticed that the lights were on, and what looked to be a dark, shadow-like figure was walking back and forth, seemingly looking for something. But I immediately knew that something was wrong. My two brothers had moved out of the house a couple months prior to this night and both of my parents were fast asleep in the bedroom that was directly next to mine. So, with this knowledge only came more fear. I had hoped that it was my dad getting up in the middle of the night wanting to work on one of his projects because he simply couldn't sleep, but that wasn't the case.

Unlike most kids, I was absolutely transfixed by what I was watching and found that I couldn't look away from the stranger in the shed despite the fact that my heart was beating in my chest as rapidly as could be. Similar to me, Nick was also unable to look away from the shed for a good minute or so. All four of our eyes watched with a waiting intensity, almost as if we expected something even more frightening to happen. Maybe this figure would turn his head ever so slightly and stare up at us through our window. Maybe he would exit the shed any moment now, and we would see who this bizarre person or whatever it was, in the flesh.

But after about a minute, we had a sort of unspoken agreement where we both decided to look away. I remember us talking about what we thought it was and what they were doing in the shed but amazingly, we were able to play a bit more of the video game for a couple of minutes before we went to look out the window again. In the massive backyard, my family and I had quite the hefty ping-pong table set up that we forgot to bring back inside once the cold weather struck, so it was left out there for months on end. And it was heavy.

When we looked outside the bedroom window once more, we saw that the ping-pong table had moved all the way to the other side of the yard. At this, Nick and I simply stared at one another, and we kept muttering "Oh my god". It was at that moment we knew that something was wrong, but we just didn't know what to do about it. I thought of waking up my parents at the time. Maybe they could've taken a good look in the backyard. But I figured that if they went to investigate and ended up finding absolutely nothing, they would've thought we were losing our minds.

So the two of us just sat in the bedroom for a good thirty minutes, watching through the window, waiting to see if the stranger was still in the backyard or if he had moved on. Was he hiding somewhere? We didn't really want to know the answer to that. After a while, Nick and I proceeded to head downstairs into the kitchen area, where we would be able to peek through a much larger window, allowing us to see almost the entirety of the backyard.

And thanks to this window, we noticed that a handful of items in the yard had been misplaced. Toy swords, baseball gloves, and pieces of firewood had all been moved around as well as the ping-pong table. The shed door, however, remained shut, but the light inside was off by the time we went downstairs. At the time, my family and I didn't have an alarm system but we thankfully always locked our doors, so Nick and I took a little bit of comfort knowing that there was no way this person could've snuck into the house.

But even still, that didn't erase all our fears - we were still terrified knowing that this entity could still be hanging around the house outside, perhaps waiting for us to go and investigate. Waiting for its prey. We all know that kids are sometimes not the brightest people on the planet, but what Nick and I did next was truly one of the dumbest things any kid could ever do. We went outside to investigate.

Nick led the way because he wanted to be the brave one which was more than fine with me. Nick crept slowly up to the shed door, where I stood a few feet back, feeling as though a hundred thousand pairs of eyes were on me, and each second that ticked by felt like an eternity. As Nick carefully pulled the shed door open, he peered inside before he took one step in. I thought the worst. Was my friend going to die in there? As a ten-year-old, I was confident that something terrible was about to happen.

A few seconds went by, and I didn't know what to do besides stand there, waiting for any sign of life from my friend. I didn't want to call out his name either, just in case this stranger was somewhere nearby, and by my voice, he would then know exactly where I was. Then, Nick thankfully steps outside of the shed, telling me that all was clear. It was an absolute wave of relief and we both felt a lot better knowing that this person wasn't still in the shed. But there was still that twinge of fear that crept into our minds. *What if he's still here? Did we miss him?*

We walked up to the porch, just about ready to head back inside and call off our all-nighter and get some much-needed rest when we heard what sounded like a calm, careful voice whisper my name. *"Calvin"*. Nick spun his head around instantly, his face and probably my face as well, contorted with a look of horror. We were really dumb kids but we weren't dumb enough to go near the source of the sound, which sounded as if it were coming from around the corner of the house. We both raced inside, locked the back door, and headed upstairs, going to bed.

The next morning, we woke up and all we could think about was what we saw in the backyard. Usually when Nick and I had a sleepover, the next morning we would spend some time playing some more video games, watching YouTube videos, and getting ready to say goodbye to one another but that morning was different. Everything felt so strange and different because everything *was* different. In a way, it kind of brought us closer together because more than ten years later, we are still talking about that night and what happened.

We even talked to my dad that morning about the incident and he insisted that he was not outside in the shed at all. My brother was sleeping at his girlfriend's house that night. So what in the world could've possibly happened? Why did this stranger head inside my shed? Was he looking for something specific? Surely he was, otherwise he wouldn't have gone inside the shed, but to this day, I have no idea what he could've been searching for.

Because Nick and I were so exhausted by the time this happened, we are also still unsure whether or not we really *did* hear my name being whispered, but we believe that it did happen because both of us heard it. Auditory hallucinations occurring in two different people at the same time would surely produce different noises. What Nick would hear and I would hear would be totally different. But we heard my name whispered at the same time, and coming from the same place.

It's been well over a decade since this incident has happened but every single time I think about it, I get more and more creeped out by it. I sometimes wonder where this stranger is now and what he's doing. Has he done the same exact thing to other people? Is he still living in the very city that I still live in to this day? These are questions I don't think I want to know the answer to. But nevertheless, this still keeps me up at night, and some part of me thinks that one day, he'll be back.

THE FACE

On August 24, 2019, in the city of Newryst, heavy rain was falling and served as a curtain call for all who were outside, trying to enjoy their last little bit of summer before the inevitable chill of Autumn air whisked through the streets. Street vendors were hauling their carts out of the rain's ferocious path, a couple walking their poodle were briskly walking with their hoods pulled over their head to block the rain's direct force, saying "Come on, Sandy! Let's get to shelter!". Meanwhile, a handful of toddlers seized the opportunity to splash in the puddles on the sidewalk, even though they weren't dressed properly, because to hell with rain boots.

And then there was Ellie Anderson, sitting in apartment, tapping a ballpoint pen against the tip of her lips, deep in thought, before eventually writing down all of her thoughts which proved to be therapeutic.

If you were to tell Ellie as early as one year ago that she would write in a journal every week just a year down the road, she would have laughed and called you stupid. Ellie thought journals were for young, love-struck pre-teen girls who couldn't help but swoon over the guy that they'd never date because he was too out of their league.

She only started writing in a journal because her therapist told her to do so. "I know you're very hesitant with the whole journal entry thing, but I think it would do you a lot of good. Please, do me a favor - just go home after our session today and write down *one* short entry. Just one", Dr. Ackmann pleaded.

"What do I have to write about that's interesting? Everything in my life is shitty, so I really don't think that writing about just how shitty it is will make anything remotely better", Ellie retorted.

But later that night, after finishing up watching a brand new episode of *Supernatural*, she found herself sitting on her couch in the middle of her living room, twiddling her fingers and looking around carelessly. Her eyes eventually fixated on an old notebook that she didn't even remember having placed on top of a dresser next to her television set, but alas, there it was.

She started writing about all of her thoughts and feelings. She found that once she picked up the pen and wrote just one sentence, every little ounce of emotion she had bottled up inside had spilled out onto the pages. Before she knew it, she had written up four entire pages.

Sure, almost all of it was incoherent ramblings that went on and on about things that didn't really seem to matter anymore, but she found that Dr. Ackmann's words were right ever since the day she recommended the journal idea. Writing down her thoughts genuinely *did* help her.

That night, she went to bed just like any other night. Except for Ellie, every night was hell. She never thought she would be envious of those who could go to bed regularly but ever since the previous year's events happened, she tosses and turns in bed for hours at a time. No matter how long she closes her eyes and tries to block out any distractions, it almost never works.

In between these states of sleeplessness, Ellie frequently has hallucinations of a man standing in her room with a featureless face repeating the words *"You did this. You did this."* over and over again.

She saw this man appear in her house on a bi-daily basis, and it was getting to the point where she simply could not take it anymore. Some part of her mind kept reminding her that this man was not real and that he was only a figment of her worst imaginations. Nobody on the face of the Earth could look like that, even in her wildest dreams.

But reason eventually gave way to insanity. Perhaps if this man hadn't come to her room to stare at her and taunt her with his words this one night, she would've let it all go. But sometimes, all it takes is for something to happen one more time in order for a person to finally snap and say "enough is enough".

Ellie knew all too well that sleep was not going to come to her that night no matter how long and hard she tried to shut her eyelids and force herself to drift off. It just wasn't going to happen. Sleep and Ellie were not a match made in heaven, but rather, hallucinations and delirium were.

Throwing her legs off the side of her bed, Ellie stalked over to the kitchen countertop where she proceeded to grab the sharpest knife in the block which happened to be a massive butcher's knife. Even though she couldn't see the man at the moment, she knew he wasn't gone. Not yet.

There she was, back pressed up against the kitchen fridge, the knife being held limply in her right hand as she swayed on her feet in a tired and dazed manner. She shut her eyes involuntarily for just a moment which then gave an opportunity for the man to appear without her noticing.

Alas, there he stood, tall in his black trench coat. His bald, featureless head seemed like it was pointed directly at her but was, in all reality, probably looking somewhere else. Ellie couldn't tell because this thing had no eyes and no nose. Even when it told Ellie *"You did this. You did this"*, it didn't have a mouth to pronounce the phrase. It was almost like the words were being translated into thin air.

Although a bit apprehensive about it, Ellie walked briskly over to the man in the dark clothing, knife at the ready, eager to finally get rid of the unwanted visitor once and for all. But as soon as she got within striking distance…

Whoosh.

The figure transformed into a cloud of black dust, which left Ellie coughing vigorously for a few seconds. The air in her apartment suddenly smelled like rotting flesh that had been left out in the cold for hours. Ellie stared out her apartment window at which point she saw the figure once more, but this time, it was standing in the middle of Cunningham Park, adjacent to her room.

Fuck this, Ellie thought. She knew that if she decided to give up now and simply head back to bed, this figure would just come back the next night to do this routine all over again, if not that *same* night. She needed to put an end to this and she needed to do it now.

But what was interesting to her at the moment was that now, it seemed as though the figure was no longer quite featureless. The man had matted dark brown hair, and she could've sworn that the man looked strangely familiar.

Ellie had read somewhere that every person you see in your dreams is somebody that you have already met in the past, or, somebody that you will meet in the future. But this man was never a part of Ellie's dreams. *Who could it be?*

Throwing on her coat and heading downstairs, Ellie opened the door and stepped out into the cold Autumn night, the city absolutely deserted except for a few taxi cabs driving by, dropping off passengers at their designated location.

Ellie stalked her way into Cunningham Park but ultimately stopped dead in her tracks. She didn't see anything suspicious at all. There was no sign of the strange man anywhere but rather, a typical view for a forest - trees scattered about, some pieces of candy wrappers and plastic grocery store bags lining the ground while a couple of lamp posts kept things illuminated.

The world had grown so incredibly silent that Ellie became apprehensive about even stepping one more foot inside the park. She thought she should be hearing *something* at that moment - maybe some pigeons or the sound of cars driving by in the night - but everything was so mute that she would've been able to hear a pin drop.

Nevertheless, she trudged deeper inward with the knife now gripped more tightly in her hand, the only sound audible to her that of her shoes kicking sidewalk under her feet.

Maybe I should just go home now, Ellie thought. There was a rumbling sensation of unease slowly building deep inside her. A feeling that refused to leave. But just as she turned around, she felt a grip as strong as an industrial press squeezing down on a piece of metal.

It was a pair of hands squeezing her throat so hard that it eventually caused Ellie's windpipe to completely give out. Ellie slowly felt the life draining from her body as her skin was turning a purplish-blue color.

The man eventually dropped Ellie to the ground, where she knelt on both knees before the man in the dark coat knelt down with her so he could be face to face with his victim. Now that she was so close to him, she could make out the figure clear as day. But the realization of who it was made it ten times worse.

It was her father.

As Mr. Anderson stared into the windows of his daughter's soul, he grabbed the knife that had since collapsed to the floor, and proceeded to stab her directly in the heart before uttering one simple phrase:

"You did this".

THE ANTIQUE STORE

Nine-year-old Isabella Newton was sitting in the backseat of her parents' 1960 Ford Country Squire fiddling with her dress, which was patterned with blue flowers all over it, while in the front seat, her father Ethan and mother Kathryn were quietly humming along to the tune of Elvis Presley's "Suspicious Minds" while driving down a lonesome road on a cold Autumn day in October 1969.

Ever since she could remember, Isabella loved going on road trips with her parents. She didn't necessarily enjoy sleeping in old wooden cabins (she usually got homesick the moment they arrived at their campsite) but rather, it was the journey that she loved.

She went to the store and ran various errands with her parents on a frequent basis so she got to sit in the back seat of their car often, but she always felt sad when it was time to head back inside their home. Isabella loved sitting and looking out the window at other passing vehicles, watching people sit on benches sharing coffees with one another, smiling faces passing by, and the blur of neon lights as they passed by various different cities and towns.

There were only ever two reasons why Ethan and Kathryn would go on road trips - to simply go camping and explore the world, or to go visit Kathryn's side of the family who resided in Blumington. Ethan's parents had passed away just five years ago, but when it happened he wasn't too terribly upset - he knew their days were numbered.

The older you get, the less time you naturally have. When Ethan's parents died, they were eighty-nine and ninety-one respectively. And while Ethan had secretly thought to himself "Why couldn't you two have just clung onto your lives a few years longer?" he knew it wasn't in their hands to control how long they lived. For all Ethan knew, he could die tomorrow. So could Kathryn. And god forbid - so could his little nine-year-old daughter Isabella who he loved more than anything else in the world.

Even just the thought of that happening made him feel horrible inside. Death was something that Ethan was incredibly scared of even though he never vocally expressed this to anybody.

He had been working as an air-compressor salesman for the past eight years and grew extremely close to one of his co-workers - John. Ethan was definitely the kind of person who got a lot of work done and didn't mess around - but whenever there were a few minutes to spare or whenever lunch break was called, Ethan and John would find themselves talking for what felt like maybe two minutes but was actually more like thirty minutes.

They would spend time asking each other questions such as

"How's the wife and kids?" and "Did you catch that Yankees game the other night?" and would tell each other stories about the various things they got up to the past weekend.

John had a wife named Jessica and a ten-year-old boy named Israel, whom he loved taking to play baseball outdoors on hot summer days. As much as Israel loved playing the sport, he had told his father that he wasn't quite ready to play in any little league quite yet. "Why not? You're an amazing player and any team that you play for would be incredibly lucky to have you", his father would say.

"One day I will, but for now, can't we just play together? Just me and you?" Isreal would ask. And although his father couldn't wait for the day to come when his son would be a part of an actual baseball team - even if it was just a little league team - he was more than happy to play ball with his son just as a small hobby. Something fun to do during a hot summer day.

After about one year of playing with his father for fun, Israel eventually joined the little league team and found himself having a blast every time he stepped out onto the field. Israel was an introvert and mostly kept to himself. He didn't have a whole lot of friends at school - he liked to stick with the ones he had ever since the start of elementary school. He was simply much too scared to approach other kids and strike up conversations with them, even if he knew that they had similar interests to him - in this instance, baseball.

Even though he was playing on a team now, he still didn't try to make any friends. Not even with his fellow teammates. He would simply show up, play ball, and head home with his father who would pepper him with praise, stating "I couldn't believe that play you made! You practically hit the ball so far out of the park it might've even gone to the moon!", which always made Israel flash a toothy grin.

John would always tell Ethan stories about how great his son was at baseball and how proud he was of him. "Truth be told, I didn't think my boy was ever going to join a team. He just doesn't like being around people too much", John would say. "But ever since he joined, he's looked so happy out there. I-It just makes me so happy to see him happy and having fun on the field".

The two work friends would spend far too much time talking back and forth about their day-to-day lives and would always leave for the day giving each other a hug and saying "See you tomorrow!". They did it every day to the point where if they didn't say it to each other their day would have felt incomplete. It would have thrown them off for the rest of the evening.

One day though, John came into work, and instead of wearing his usual happy face and can-do attitude, he came in looking miserable. Ethan had been working there just as long as John had - eight full years - and not once had he seen this look on his friend's face. He had seen John have his bad days - everybody had those - but the face he was wearing today was not just any ordinary bad day face. Ethan knew the instant he saw him that something was deeply wrong.

Instead of beating around the bush, when Ethan approached

John, he blurted out, "Hey man. What's the matter? You don't look so good". To which John simply hung his head low and started to cry, which Ethan had never seen him do before. If the devastating look on John's face wasn't enough to scare Ethan before, this act of pouring salty discharge from his eyes certainly was.

Ethan gave his friend a hug and asked him "What happened? Is everything alright?". Ethan was praying to God that nothing bad had happened but he immediately thought the worst. *What if Israel had died? Or maybe Jessica? No, that can't be. Maybe his son just got booted off the baseball team. But if that's the case, then he wouldn't be crying this much. Right? Right...?*

"I-I-" John stammered through his tears. "I don't know how to say this", he said.

Ethan, trying to console him, "It's okay. Just take your time." Eventually, John got it off his chest. He said the words and as soon as he said them, Ethan knew why he had been crying so hard. He knew why he had a terribly upset look on his face - like his heart had been ripped out of his chest. And he knew that nothing was ever going to be the same.

"I have stage four cancer, Ethan", John blurted out. "I have fucking *cancer*. That's exactly how my dad died when I was a kid and now that's how I'm going to die too. I'm going to fucking *die*," he said through a puddle of tears.

John didn't even need to look up to know that his best friend was already starting to tear up as well. Ethan knew that cancer was a terrible disease but was shocked at just how sudden it could all be. And because it was already in its fourth stage, he also knew that this was it. There was no saving him no matter how much he could try. His best friend of eight years was going to die soon and there was nothing that could be done to prevent it from happening. It was set in stone.

The next three months at work were a lot more dourer than they usually were for obvious reasons. Everybody at work found out about the news and it was clear that everybody had been affected by the disheartening news. Most people have a few enemies at work. People that they can't stand and people that they argue with occasionally. But everybody loved John. He was always a friendly face to everyone and constantly went out of his way to make sure that everybody was having a good day even when he was absolutely swamped with work.

"Hey Este, you want me to get you a coffee refill?", "I can stay behind work today and help you finish up", were just a few of the things he would say to his fellow co-workers to make sure that they were happy and taken care of. Everybody loved seeing him around the building but now they knew that he wasn't going to be in the building for too much longer.

And although John was best friends with Ethan, their conversations never had the same flair or energy that they once had. Everything felt so melancholy and bleak. Even conversations about food or new clothes they had bought felt strained and hard to get out of their mouths.

John even found it difficult to talk about his son's baseball games anymore, which hurt John himself deeply. Before, he was able to watch his son's games with a huge smile on his face, cheering him on as he swung the bat and ran to second, third, and fourth base but he found it physically painful to do that now.

He would try his best to cheer him on but it was never the same. Not only did he burst into uproarious coughing fits that would cause everybody to turn their head and give him a disgusted look, but he felt mentally incapable of cheering him on the same way he used to not too long ago, even though it felt like that old life of his was years in the past.

Israel knew that his dad was dying, too, and the fact that John knew that Israel knew about his days being numbered shattered his heart. Israel had always been a daddy's boy and had spent nearly every passing second with his father whenever he was home from work. He had two or three friends at school that he would talk to, but his dad was always his best friend. The person he could tell anything. The person he found easy to joke around with and play ball together and make food together. Ever since the news was broken though, Israel looked distraught, understandably.

One night, while at the dinner table with John and his mother Jessica, Israel had said something that caused everybody in the room to freeze. The air in the room was terribly uncomfortable and there was a lingering feeling of dread and unease lurking throughout. "Daddy... I don't want you to die. Please don't die", he said.

Jessica, who had been twirling her spaghetti on her fork just a moment ago, had now dropped it on the table in surprise and upset. "I-Uh-" she stammered before composing herself, finally finding the words. "Daddy's not going to die. Okay? He's going to get all the treatment he needs, and after he's all better, you two can go play baseball and get a nice big ice cream cone together. How does that sound?" she asked. But instead of answering with an enthusiastic "Okay, mom!", he simply stood up out of his chair, leaving his dinner half-eaten, and walked upstairs, going to bed early.

Both adults simply looked at each other and hung their heads low in solemnity. There were no amount of words in the dictionary that could break the tension right at this moment and make everything feel okay. John wished he could have kept his cancer diagnosis a secret from his son but he knew that would have been impossible. Someone, somehow, would have brought it up and that would have made things a whole lot worse. "Why didn't you tell me about it, Dad? Are you gonna be okay?" he could picture his son asking.

Plus if neither he nor Jessica ever told Israel about the illness, and John had simply passed away out of the blue, Israel would have been even more hurt. Having his dad ripped away from this Earth in seemingly the blink of an eye. He knew that no matter what he did with his diagnosis - no matter when he told his son and no matter what way he told it to him - it was going to be heartbreaking and painful.

Weeks went on and on and Ethan was slipping at work slowly but surely. His boss Kevin had always told him that he was the best asset to the entire team. He was a hard-working man, and no matter what issues faced him, he pushed them aside and got the job done on a daily basis. But now, he found himself feeling unmotivated practically every day. On the days when he was supposed to be driving to meet up with clients outside of the city, he found himself doing that less and less. He would see a few people a week and wouldn't sell nearly as many air compressors as he would have about a year or so ago.

Nearly every client thought he was an awful salesman. He would go to meet up with them in a coffee shop and he would constantly stutter over his words or simply not say enough in order to convince the potential buyer.

"So... uh... yeah, no, this air compressor here is really good and..." he wouldn't be able to finish his sentence. Before, he was able to sell these things like it was no problem. It was as easy for him to do as handing over a lollipop to a toddler and asking them to say "Please" if they wanted to get it. He almost never had trouble making a sale unless the customer was just an uptight jackass.

It got so bad that Kevin eventually called John into his office to question the matter. "What's been going on with you recently? You used to be my best salesman - everybody would buy from us when you gave the proposition - but now, you struggle with every sale you do. Customers have said that they're surprised you're even a part of our team because they say that you don't know what you're doing", Kevin said.

Ethan simply exhaled quietly before saying "I-I just... I'm having a really tough time. You have to understand that my best friend has terminal cancer and I feel like he's going to die any day now. It's all I can think about. Even when I try everything in my power to take my mind off of it - even just momentarily - I can't seem to do it."

"So, what are you trying to say? That you quit?" Kevin asked. "No, no, not at all", Ethan answered. "Just… All I ask is that you try to bear with me for a little while longer. I'll do my best to get the job done like always but, I just need you to understand what I've been going through for the past few months. It's hard when you know you're about to lose one of the closest people in your life", Ethan finished.

Although Kevin was getting more and more flustered on a daily basis, he knew that letting go of Ethan would be a colossal mistake and one that he didn't know how to bounce back from. Ethan wasn't being the best salesman as of late, but he knew firsthand how great he was deep down inside.

"Okay Ethan, I'm not going to make any bad decisions today. But, seriously, please do everything that you can to get the job done. It's genuinely disheartening to see you so…" he paused, searching for the right words. "So… disheveled. I know how hard things must be for you at the moment, and have been for the past few months. I believe in you. Now get out there and show me your best", Kevin said.

Weeks went by and Ethan was slowly but surely doing better, while it was clear that John was at the worst point of his life. Kevin had only kept John on as a part of the team because he didn't want to be the asshole that fired the guy with terminal cancer. John was practically doing nothing at work these days and still getting paid for it.

Every day John would clock out of work, drive home through the streets of Newryst and stare off into space while worming his way through traffic. He paid so little attention to the road that even he was surprised he had yet to get into a collision.

When he walked inside, the aroma of Jessica's cooking would immediately waft into his nostrils and would instantly make him feel a whole lot better. Most men say it to their wives - *Honey, you're the best cook in the world* - but John legitimately meant it.

He had always considered himself to be quite the food connoisseur - he had eaten foods from at least one-hundred different restaurants - different types of food such as pasta, pizza, fish, sushi, chicken, burgers, squid, etc. - and yet no cook he had ever come across had made a dish as mean as his wife.

Grilled lemon chicken, garlic, and basil seasoned potatoes, fresh green beans, and rolls that were baked in a buttery, flaky crust were just a few of the items that Jessica was preparing for the three of them that evening. Food was a magical thing for their family.-It would simply make all of their worries dissipate - even for just a few minutes - as soon as they started to dig in.

They especially went all out for Christmas. Although they were not religious, each one of them looked forward to Christmas Day more than any other day of the year. They all agreed that there was this indescribable, special quality to it that made them all feel warm and happy inside.

A twenty-five-pound golden brown turkey cooked in the oven for at least seven hours, creamy mashed potatoes, roasted potatoes with garlic and basil seasoning, stuffing, pickled onions, cranberry bites, buttery rolls, and slices of cheesecake for dessert were just a few of the items they typically ate every holiday to go along with the feelings of joy received from opening and giving presents and seeing their loved ones.

John sat down that night and proceeded to eat every last piece of food on his plate and Israel proceeded to do the same but at a considerably slower rate. John had been the same way as a kid - he ate slower than a snail moved.

Later that night, after John had gone and kissed Israel goodnight, he strode down into his bedroom where he joined Jessica in the bed. "How are you feeling, babe?" she asked him. "I'm trying my best, day by day. It's all still so hard but I'm doing my best. For you, Israel and my job", John answered.

"I know you are honey, and I appreciate you so much. Israel does too. More than you'll ever know. I don't want you thinking for a second that you're not doing enough for your family because you are. You're the best husband I could have ever asked for, and you're the best daddy to Israel you could possibly be", Jessica stated.

At this, John smiled but then exhaled a long sigh. "I really hope so. I know how difficult this is on him, and I know it must be equally as difficult for you, too", he said and brushed his hand through her long blonde hair. The two simply stared into each other's eyes while laying in bed for several minutes before a tear started to form in John's eye.

"What's the matter, John? Is everything alright?", Jessica asked.
"I just... I don't want to die", John stated.

Jessica was usually exceptionally good at consoling people and telling them that everything was going to be alright, but Jessica knew that her husband was going to die. There was no amount of crying or consoling that could be done to save him. If his doctors had caught the cancer growing in his pancreas earlier, then perhaps they could have treated it and John could have lived a long and happy life. But this was not going to happen.

"I know, babe. I know. Just...", Jessica struggled for words. "Just know that even after you're gone, we will never, *ever*, stop loving you. You're always going to be a part of me. You're always going to be a part of Israel", she finished.

She was going to leave it at that, but breathed out, and said "When he grows up, he is going to be an amazing man just like you are", she almost said *were* but didn't, "and it's all thanks to you. You are an incredible father to him. He looks up to you like you're some superhero or something", she said.

"Which I'm not", John said and managed to laugh, which caused Jessica to laugh and smile along. Seeing John finally laugh - *truly* laugh from the bottom of his heart and not a forced laugh - nearly brought her to tears.

"To him, you are. You're better than Superman to our boy. You're the best role model to him and even when he's thirty, forty, hell, even *fifty* years old, he will never forget you and all of the things you did for him", she concluded.

At that, John smiled wider and looked like he was finally at peace, and whispered "I love you, Jessica", to which his wife replied, "I love you too, John."

*

A few months later, Ethan woke up, brushed his teeth, and was about to leave for work when Kathryn urged him to quickly eat before he headed out for the day. "Please hun, even if it's just a granola bar, you have to eat something. I don't want you to be going the whole day without any food in your stomach", she pressed.

Ethan simply smiled and said "Okay, okay, fine. You win", and reached into the cupboard, taking two chocolate chip protein-infused granola bars, opening one and placing the other inside of his work bag.

Before he stepped outside, he kissed Kathryn goodbye and went over to his daughter Isabella, kissing her on the forehead and saying "Take care of mommy for me, okay?".

Every day that Ethan drove to work he would find it one of the most relaxing parts of his day. The roads were usually relatively empty except for a few cars that were also more than likely on their way to work from nine to five.

Ethan always loved driving through rainy weather like today's, even though it would sometimes make his car slide around the highway.

He casually looked out the windshield to see the city passing by him and the birds cawing throughout the air, living their lives peacefully. *I wish I could live as free as a bird,* he thought. After driving for a solid twenty minutes, he finally idled his car into the parking lot, grabbed his briefcase, and headed inside to work for the day.

Immediately, a terrible feeling rose up within his stomach. The building he worked in was full of cubicles and people chatting away, some lingering around the water cooler or coffee machine, but today was drastically different.

A large number of the cubicles didn't have a soul behind the desk, and there wasn't anybody in sight. Ethan proceeded to walk slowly throughout the building, craning his neck around the corners where he finally walked up to the break room and saw every single employee inside.

He turned the doorknob and headed in, where he fully expected there to have been an impromptu meeting about new potential clients or a new shipment coming in, but that couldn't have been further from the truth.

When Ethan straddled inside the room, Kevin and the rest of the staff looked at him with droopy eyes and their entire demeanor looking completely drained. "Uh… what's going on?" Ethan asked nobody in particular.

It was Kevin who decided to answer his question. "I think it's best if you find a seat and sit down first", Kevin commented, to which Ethan obliged.

Kevin cleared his thought and paced back and forth before finally stopping. He took one long breath and said "Ethan… I don't know how I'm going to break this to you, but", he paused, " John passed away in his sleep last night".

*

As soon as the words left Kevin's mouth, Ethan immediately lost his breath. He actually stood up and proceeded to pace the room back and forth, each breath of his getting heavier and faster.

"Calm down, Ethan", Kevin stated. "I can't fucking *calm down!*", Ethan yelled louder than he had intended. Everybody in the room had wide eyes now - they had never seen Ethan yell or even mildly lose his temper, although they knew that when Ethan found out about the news of John's passing, his reaction wasn't going to be laid back.

"How the fuck do you expect me to calm down after you've told me that my best friend is dead?", Ethan asked the room. It wasn't just Kevin that he was mad at now. The whole room was looking at him like he was acting out of line, but Ethan didn't care.

"How do-" Ethan started but eventually stopped, not knowing what words were going to flow out of his mouth next.

"Look... Ethan. I know how close John was to you, and so I just wanted to say that I am sorry for your loss", Kevin said. Upon hearing this, tears were quickly beginning to form in Ethan's eyes and were slowly trickling down his cheeks, before he eventually sat back down in his chair with his hands covering his face.

"John's passing is obviously a tremendous loss for all of us here. Not only was he a terrific employee for this company - always showing up to work on time despite his illness, showing kindness and empathy to others, and getting the job done right - but he was a member of our family. We all loved him and will continue to love him in the wake of his death".

Hearing the words "John's passing" and "his death" made Ethan realize that his best friend in the world really *was* gone. He had desperately hoped that maybe there was some awful misunderstanding. Perhaps Kevin had been talking about something entirely unrelated to his best friend John Rothe, and maybe it was another guy named John that had died. But with each passing second, Ethan knew that it was *his* John that Kevin had been talking about.

"There is going to be a celebration of John's life held inside this building next Friday, so please bring food and drinks and bring as many people as possible to help remember our friend", Kevin stated.

Nobody in the entire room had anything to say - they all hung there silent as if speaking any word aloud would cause their worlds to shatter - before Kevin eventually broke the silence by stating "You may now get back to work", which caused every employee to file out of the room and head back to their cubicles, except for Ethan who was still sitting in his chair with his hands covering his face.

"Ethan… are you alright? Do you need anything at all?" Kevin asked him. He knew the question was probably a silly one - how can you console somebody after they just got confirmation that their best friend of nearly a decade had died? - but he felt like it should be said anyway. Just in case there was some way to help him relax and feel better. Even just temporarily.

"I don't know. Just-" Ethan began before pausing to find the right words. "Can I take today off? I can come in tomorrow, I just think I'll need today to myself to relax and rest. This is all just… so much", he choked on the last word.

Kevin sort of knew that this was coming already, but now that he heard the words spoken aloud, he was admittedly a bit upset.

Ethan had always shown up to work every single day and was a valuable asset to the company, and Kevin was worried that by him not being at work today - on a Friday of all days which was typically the busiest day of the week for them - there wouldn't be as much work done in general.

Because he had already told Ethan if there was anything he could do to help, he answered him with "Sure, I guess. Just, uh-" he paused, "maybe give me a call at the end of the day or something. See how you're feeling then and if you're up for coming back to work on Monday morning".

Ethan was genuinely surprised that his boss had let him take the day off. He was sort of well-known around the office for not letting anybody take time away from work no matter what the circumstances were.

One time, one of his co-workers named Sam, had told Kevin that he needed to take a few weeks off since his mother had just died but Kevin denied the request, stating "There's work to be done, and I expect you to do it".

Upon hearing his boss's approval, Ethan actually muttered a quick "Oh! Uh-" but recovered quickly, stating "Thanks, Kevin. I'll let you know how everything is going this weekend and what my status is by Monday". Kevin simply give him a hand wave as if to say *Okay, you can go now.*

As he was walking out of the front door, he quickly turned his head around to see all of his co-workers sitting at their cubicles, they too not being able to get much work done at all. Some people were simply sitting in front of their computers with their hands on their faces, barely able to even open a web page.

When Ethan walked outside in the Autumn air he felt an intense shiver go up to his spine. It wasn't because the air was cool - it was but not cool enough to get shivers - but rather, it was the first time he had gotten fresh air ever since the news was broken to him just moments ago.

Even though he was glad to have gotten the day off and in turn the rest of the weekend, he dreaded having to drive back home now. The road that connected his workplace to his house was always backed up no matter what time of the day it was.

One time he was out late with a friend of his at around 11:00 pm and it was as busy as it usually was during lunch-time rush hour.

Ethan spent the next couple of days at home laying on the couch and watching some movies with Kathryn and Isabella playing around with her new favorite toy in the world - a balloon. She would ask her parents to inflate it for her and after it was gigantic, she would whack it up against the walls inside their home - Ethan actually thought it looked a little fun.

But it was clear to everybody in that household that Ethan was going through hell and wasn't going to be his usual cheery self for a long while. They didn't know when they would see that side of him again, but they knew that they would in due time. In the meantime, they were willing to do whatever it took to cheer him up.

On Sunday night, Kathryn even made his favorite meal on planet Earth - what they all deemed "Birthday Soup" when she would make him a gigantic pot of chicken noodle soup every year for his birthday that was loaded with delicious white meat chicken breast, cooked carrot slices, celery, onions, and potatoes. He often got stomach cramps after eating it simply because he ate too much.

And while he certainly did brandish a huge smile upon smelling the soup cooking in the kitchen and was obviously enjoying himself as he shoveled spoonfuls into his mouth, after dinner was over he still looked out of it and not himself.

Just before Ethan was about to go up to bed with Kathryn and tuck Isabella in for the night, the home phone rang, and immediately, he knew who it was.

Their home phone got plenty of calls each and every day - faraway family members saying "hello" or calling to say somebody had died, friends checking up on Ethan and his family, and of course, scammers. They took up about ninety percent of their incoming calls.

Ah, fuck, Ethan thought as soon as he heard the phone ring. *What am I going to say? I can't go back tomorrow. Shit.* But he picked up anyway and sure enough, the familiar drawl of Kevin's voice spoke on the other end of the line.

"Hey Ethan, just figured I'd give you a quick call to see how you're holding up", his boss had said. Even though Ethan promised Kevin that he'd call him by the end of the weekend, he sort of forgot and was a little bit pissed off about the entire situation. His best friend had died and yet here Ethan was getting pestered by his boss about how he was feeling.

He felt like yelling over the phone *"Of course I'm not fucking okay! I'll quit this shitty fucking job right now! So leave me alone!"* but deep down he knew that probably wasn't the best idea. Especially since his family definitely needed money and he didn't want to be one of those dads that were out of work, struggling to make ends meet while his family was starving and about to lose their house.

Ethan wasn't going to bullshit Kevin and tell him that everything was all fine and dandy - he was going to tell him the truth as much as he could. "Look... I, uh-" he paused momentarily, "I'm not feeling too great. I'm sorry. I know you're relying on me to come back to work tomorrow and I know that I should have called you earlier in the day to give you more of a heads up, but honestly" he paused once more not wanting to say the words. He was worried to do it.

"I don't think I'm going to be able to come into work tomorrow. Or Tuesday", he finished.

He was almost positive Kevin was going to blurt out and give him hell, saying something like "I don't care! You better get your damn ass to work tomorrow morning or you're fired - no if's, and's, or but's", but instead, there was a long silence on the other end of the phone that actually caused more panic and upset within Ethan than there would've been if Kevin had simply told him that.

After a while, the silence became so unbearable that Ethan had to speak up once more. "I know you're counting on me to come back to work soon and I know you're probably going to fire me but I'm asking you... please just be patient with me. You know how much I need this job and you know that I need to keep it for Kathryn and for Isabella."

Finally, Kevin said something on the other end that surprised Ethan. He simply said in an annoyed but soft tone, "Ethan...", almost as if to say *Come on, man, really? I know you're struggling but this is just unacceptable.* "I know. I know this doesn't look good for me and I know that I'm probably the least valuable member of the company at this point but just give me a few days at the most. Please", Ethan begged.

"Okay, look. I'll give you a few more days but that's it. You can't keep doing this. What am I paying you for? To sit around at home and wallow in your tears?", Kevin asked, and as soon as he said it he was full of regrets. "I'm sorry, I just… Get some rest and I'll call you in a couple of days. Okay?", Kevin questioned.

"Yes, of course. Thank you. Have a good night", Ethan answered back to which Kevin replied "You too", and hung up the phone. The next couple of days went by in a blur although Ethan still wasn't feeling himself.

It was starting to finally take a bit of a toll on Kathryn and Isabella was getting a little bit upset too. Not because of John's death but because she had to constantly see her dad depressed on a daily basis. She just wasn't used to it, but now that she saw him with his head hung low every day, it was now starting to get to her and affect her negatively.

Ethan was lying in bed one morning when Kathryn proceeded to yell up the stairs "Ethan! Phone!", to which Ethan was praying to God that it wasn't Kevin. *For fuck's sake, what do you want this early in the morning you asshole.*

With sleep still in his eye, Ethan proceeded to get up out of bed, quickly throw on a house robe, and rush downstairs where he saw Kathryn holding up the phone to her ear and when she caught sight of her husband, said into the other line, "Okay, here he is".

Before Ethan answered it, he mouthed the words "Who is it?" to Kathryn, to which she mouthed back "It's Kevin". He sort of already had a feeling that's who it was but wanted to make sure just in case his whole entire day was about to be ruined for nothing. If it was anybody but Kevin, his day would have been totally fine.

The past couple of times Kevin had called their home phone, Ethan had answered and talked to his boss in an apologetic tone but this time, he finally gave up. "What?" he called into the phone, which caused Kathryn to look worried. *He's going to lose his job*, she thought.

It turns out, she thought correctly.

She didn't even need to hear what was coming out of Kevin's mouth on the other end of the line to know that her husband had just got booted from his job. "Look, Ethan, I was thinking about this a lot since our last phone call a couple of days ago and I've just come to the conclusion that this job isn't going to be the right fit for you", Kevin said.

Ethan had always hated that term - "this job isn't the right fit for you" - almost like working at a job was trying on a pair of shoes that were a bit too large for you.

When he used to work at a grocery store in his twenties, the manager fired him for being too slow stocking the shelves and said "I'm sorry to say this to you Ethan - I really am. You're a young man and you've got a big future ahead of you, but working here… this just isn't the right fit for you".

Isabella was sitting in the massive table chair that was way too big for her, eating a piece of French Toast that her mother had just cooked for her when she asked her, "Mommy, who is Daddy talking to?"

"Oh, he's just talking to his boss right now honey", Kathryn answered. She hoped her daughter would leave it at that, but that wasn't the case. *Kids will be kids.* "Why is his boss talking to him? Daddy isn't supposed to be working today", she said.

Kathryn replied "I know, honey. He's not working today, don't worry. He'll have plenty of time to play around with you today. Maybe we can go out for ice cream later or something" she suggested. *We'll have plenty of time to do whatever we want today because Daddy doesn't have a job anymore* she felt like saying but ultimately didn't.

"Come on, Kevin!", Ethan suddenly yelled which startled Isabella and made her tear up a little bit, causing Kathryn to hurry over and give her a kiss on the forehead. "I just don't understand why you're doing this! You told me that I could have a few days off and then come back to work and now *this* is what you're trying to do?", Ethan said back into the phone, trying not to lose his temper but wasn't doing a good job of it.

"I know I told you that but, the more I kept thinking about it, the quicker I came to the conclusion that this just isn't going to work out. I'm sorry, Ethan. I know John's passing has been hard on you and I know that you've been struggling but you can't miss work like that and now you won't be able to show up to work.", Kevin said while Ethan listened intently to every single syllable.

"I do want to thank you, however, for all of the years you put in for us. No matter what happens today, I want you to know how much I appreciate what you've done for me and the business in the past few years", he finished.

"You have *no* idea what it's like to lose someone close to you, do you?" Ethan shouted. "No, you don't! Because if you did, then you wouldn't be treating me like a piece of shit and throwing me off to the side like I'm not responsible for making your company successful in the first place! I don't kn-" he started but Kevin hung up the line.

Ethan simply stood in place, not having a clue what to do next. Kathryn looked very distraught and walked up to him slowly and carefully, placing one hand on his shoulder and saying "It's okay babe. You'll find something else, I know you will. I know it". Then, Ethan started to cry uncontrollably as Kathryn embraced him into the biggest and most loving hug she had ever given anybody.

Although he knew what his wife was saying was correct, Ethan still couldn't help but feel completely hopeless and useless at that moment. Even though he pressed forward in the face of evil and despair, things didn't necessarily improve from that day on.

*

The next few weeks of Ethan's life felt like the longest he had ever gone through. He drove around, business to business, handing out resumes, hoping that somebody would give him a call back, but few places did.

"Oh, honey keep your head held high. You're going to get something soon, I can just feel it in my bones. You've never been one to *not* find work. Just keep applying to everywhere you can find", Kathryn said. "Even to places that don't advertise that they're hiring".

He got so hopeless that he went and applied to the local McDonald's as a cashier which made him feel like shit inside. *How the hell do I go from being an air compressor salesman to a potential McDonald's employee? You're supposed to work your way up in the world, not the other way around.*

On one chilly morning, Ethan awoke and started to read the daily newspaper that they got delivered and immediately flipped to the job listings at the very back. He usually ended up reading the entire paper front to back but times were different now.

If he didn't get a job soon, his entire family was going to struggle. *My family isn't going to have enough food on the table. We're going to lose our house.*

Some of the advertised jobs were ones that he had already applied to but never heard back from, such as a hotel manager at the local Best Western, a customer service representative at a bookstore called Planet Novel, and even the McDonald's that was about a five-minute walk, with the advert reading "URGENTLY HIRING! ARE YOU LOOKING FOR A PART-TIME OR FULL-TIME JOB? COME ON BY TO THE McDONALD'S ON 525 KARSBURY ROAD, SW."

Urgently hiring, my ass Ethan thought. Just as he was about to give up on the paper's listings, one he had never seen before caught his eye and looked enticing.

"NEWRYST ANTIQUES: We specialize in finding the rarest and most valuable collectibles in the world! Do you have an item that you believe is rare / valuable / or just worth a few extra dollars? Come on down to our location at 129 Knope Street SE!"

Then, he noticed the job position:

"We are currently HIRING for a FULL-TIME sales representative and management position! Duties include communicating with customers and fulfilling their shopping or vending needs, the occasional dusting of display cases and non-fragile items, operating the cash register at the front kiosk, and helping to open and close shop at the beginning and the end of the day. If you feel you are a good fit for this job, please drop by any time during operating hours with your resume and we will get back to you as soon as possible!"

HOURS OF OPERATION:
  Mon: 8am-8pm

Tues: 8am-8pm
Wed: 8am-8pm
Thurs: 8am-8pm
Fri: 8am-8pm
Sat: 10am-6pm
Sun: 10am-6pm

Usually, Ethan liked to finish up his morning coffee and breakfast before heading out for the day, but he knew that nowadays he had to take every step possible if it meant he may end up getting a job. Not only was Newryst Antiques about a five or six-minute drive from his house, he genuinely liked antiques and enjoyed collecting them occasionally.

When he was a kid himself, his father would collect coins and some action figures and eventually ended up putting them all on display in their city's local antique store.

Every other week, Ethan's father would go down to the store with him to see if any of the items from their case had sold, and more often than not, something did - albeit something small such as a coin or a newspaper clipping from decades past - which always excited Ethan. What was once theirs now belonged in the hands of somebody else.

The entire process of buying and selling was deeply interesting to him. He always had fond memories of antique stores and collecting ever since his youngest years.

When he approached the front door of the house and placed his shoes on, ready to exit and go apply with his resume, Kathryn called out "Where are you going, hun?" to which he simply replied "Job application" before closing the door behind him on the way out. Kathryn had always admired how driven her husband was.

Some people in this situation would simply call it quits and try to live off of the government or mooch off their parents even in their thirties or forties.

As soon as Ethan pulled his vehicle into the parking lot of Newryst Antiques, he found himself stunned by just how massive the building was. It wasn't as big as a shopping mall but it was certainly the largest antique store Ethan's eyes had ever come across. It was practically the size of a typical grocery store which came as a shock to him.

Although he loved going to their local antique store as a child with his father, he had only ever stepped foot inside of smaller buildings that housed antiques. Ethan never knew such as a massive antique store could even exist.

Ethan was planning on applying for the management job but would also settle for a regular employee or sales job instead if it were offered to him. Admittedly though, he was worried about how he was going to manage such a gigantic building probably stacked full of antiques if he landed the position.

When he walked inside the building, Ethan was immediately overwhelmed by the number of collectibles that lined the inside.

At least one hundred display cases were filled with numerous items such as old newspapers, action figures, weapons, cups, stereos, turntables, vases, etc. No matter where you looked inside Newryst Antiques, you were destined to find something of interest.

There was an entire area inside that was dedicated to old Coca-Cola memorabilia which included a vintage gas pump with the iconic logo on it, vintage bottle caps, tee-shirts, hats, and even sneakers. The interior of the story was a smoky mahogany brown and was lined with linoleum carpets and yellow overhead lights illuminated the entire building.

About twenty customers were inside the store when Ethan was inside, couples walking hand in hand taking a gander at all the expensive collectibles on display, kids running around with their parents trailing behind urging "Don't knock anything over!" all while the store's two owners Jerome and Phillip stood behind the large glass countertop near the front entrance with welcoming smiles on their faces, ones that looked almost too good to be true.

They would typically follow customers around the store every once in a while if they took too long, immediately thinking that they were stealing something.

But they always made sure to approach their customers friendly and with a grin, no matter if they had suspicions of them or not. They wanted to be as welcoming as possible but it ended up creeping some customers out.

Ethan approached Jerome with his resume, and said "Hey

there, just dropping off a resume. I noticed in the newspaper this morning that you're hiring for a sales representative and management position here".

Jerome genuinely looked surprised to see that somebody was interested in applying at the store. "Oh, uh-, he stalled. "Here, let me take a look at this later on and we'll give you a call".

Ethan started to walk down to the exit door with an unsure feeling when Jerome suddenly hollered "Hey! I have a question for you!", which caused Ethan to retrace his steps. *I couldn't have gotten the job* already, *could I?* "I'm just wondering - what about this job do you think you'd like? Why do you want to work here?"

This caught Ethan by surprise. He had walked into the store completely ready to answer any and all questions by now that he was being asked upfront, his brain jammed and he was visibly stunned. "Well, I, uh... I guess I've just always liked antiques".

At this, Jerome simply stared at him for five seconds but to Ethan, it felt more like five minutes. Plus, Jerome had intense eye contact - Ethan had always made sure to look people in the eye when talking to them, but he found it difficult to look into this man's eyes for more than a few seconds.

"So," Jerome was saying as he was chewing a bite of an apple, "you want to be a sales rep or a manager?". Ethan immediately replied "Manager" way too quickly, making it seem like it was the only position he was interested in which is why he added abruptly "Or sales rep".

"Well, if you became a manager here, you'd definitely have plenty of work to do. This ain't no small store as you can obviously see", he started waving his hands around. "I've had a couple of guys - just sales reps - start working here and they just thought the place was too big. Plus, we have gone through about three different managers, each one of them left us because the building was too much for them to handle".

Okay, it's not that *big* Ethan was thinking of saying but decided not to. He didn't want to sound cocky or too assured of himself. He knew that if he did that, Jerome would sense an inauthentic quality to him that he didn't want to be seen. So he simply said, "Yeah, it sure is a big building but I'm sure it's nothing I can't handle".

It was a simple answer but it was one that Jerome obviously was glad to hear as, as soon as Ethan spoke the words, a subtle smile started to crane up Jerome's face.

"You really think so, eh?", Jerome looked down at the resume Ethan had handed to him moments ago. "I take it you're Ethan then?" he asked.

"Yes, sir", Ethan replied. "Well, Ethan - I never do this with anybody but", he paused and started scratching his head. "How about we make a deal here?" he asked.

This instantly worried Ethan but also excited him at the same time. It worried him because he hoped the deal wasn't too outrageous to fulfill but was excited because it certainly seemed to him that Jerome was interested in having him become a part of the Newryst Antiques family.

"I'm thinking what we can do is start you off as a sales rep and if the months go by and we really like you, then we can bump you up to a management position".

Really? Wow, thank you so much! Ethan almost exclaimed before he caught himself.

"Okay, yeah, I think that sounds like a fair deal", he finally said before he extended his arm outward to which Jerome shook it firmly with a smile on his face, saying "Welcome to the Newryst Antiques team".

"I'm glad to be a part of the team! When do I start?" Ethan asked. "Hmm… how does tomorrow morning at 8 am sound? Is that okay with you?" Jerome propositioned. "Yes, tomorrow morning works great! I'm looking forward to coming in", Ethan answered.

The following day, Ethan came in for his first day at his new job and found himself a natural in the position of sales representative.

He would wander the halls of the gigantic antique mall and come across customers who were usually dumbfounded at the number of items that were stored in the glass cases that adorned the walls.

Surprisingly, he noticed that customers rarely purchased anything when they stopped to have a peek inside. They would simply wander the halls with their hands in their pockets, slowly approaching various display cases filled with ancient relics and collectibles, craning their necks downward to get a better look at them before moving on to the next case.

Of course, there were a few people that purchased an item - usually, something remarkably small such as a teacup or an old doll - dolls always gave Ethan the creeps - but the number of customers that would buy items that would make big bucks were few and far between.

Gratefully, whenever somebody did buy something expensive, it seriously helped their funds and overall earnings for the business.

There were a number of items for sale in the store that had a price tag on them asking for a few thousand dollars - the most expensive of which, an antique gas pump from the 1930s with an asking price of $50,000 - but while Ethan had the occasional customer that bought a teacup, he would, every once in a while, get a customer who would approach the front desk with a thousand dollar item in their hands.

Jerome and Phillip's eyes would always bug out of their head and crack humongous grins when they saw the pricey item in question.

"Holy shit, Jerome! Look! That guy's bringing up the old .38 revolver! Does he know how expensive that is? Did he read the price tag carefully?" Phillip would ask. "Well I'm assuming he did otherwise he wouldn't be approaching the desk while pulling out his wallet", Jerome retorted.

The man did end up buying the $1,000 pistol but had a noticeably upset look on his face.

He wanted the pistol which is why he bought it, but he also realized that he just spent one thousand dollars on a pistol that he was just going to put up for display in his home. It wasn't necessarily buyer's remorse, it was more like knowing you bought something you really wanted but also knowing that you're a thousand bucks poorer.

Months went by and Ethan found that he was mostly a natural to the job, which struck him as weird considering how he had never worked in a building such as this one at any point in his life. He did have plenty of sales experience, however, which he assumed is where he got most of his strengths from.

Not to mention that he finally got the management position after Jerome and Phillip watched him go to work and interact with customers like a natural. They simply couldn't comprehend the sheer simplicity but smooth way of dealing business Ethan had about him, which is why Jerome called him into their office one day.

Ethan was convinced that he was about to get fired. *Ah, fuck. This is the last thing I need. I finally have a steady job, I'm able to pay for groceries for the whole family. Just when things were finally starting to lo-*

"Alright, Ethan, how 'bout you pull up a chair and take a seat for a few minutes?" Jerome asked. If Ethan's suspicions about being fired weren't high enough already, now they were skyrocketing. He was just about to say "I'm sorry I wasn't a good fit for the company" when Jerome started speaking again, breaking the silence that to Ethan, felt unbearable.

"Okay, so… how do I begin?" Jerome started. "Phillip and I have been running this place together for the past ten years and we like to think we know what we're doing here", he continued. Ethan had no idea where this was going but, still, his worries did not dissipate.

"We have interacted with customers and still do on a daily basis, but I gotta say… Phillip and I have seen you interact with customers for a while now and we can't believe it", he said and took a couple of seconds to pause.

Jerome was barely looking at Ethan's expression which was good for him because he knew he looked like an absolute fool. He had a million different thoughts racing through his head at the moment and he knew that the expression on his face was most likely both comical and confused and sad.

"You have just… an incredible way of dealing with customers. You handle all their questions and concerns, you always come up with solutions, and most importantly, you get the job done", Jerome finally finished. Much to his own surprise, Ethan didn't exhale a breath of fresh air or a slight smile when Jerome finished his statement.

He had worked himself up into such a mental frenzy of

possibilities of why he was about to get fired that what Jerome just said wasn't even a possibility in his head.

Eventually, Jerome grinned wide which, in turn, caused Ethan to, at long last, flash a toothy smile who then laughed heartily and said "Well, thank you. I always try to do my best, so I'm glad to hear that I succeed".

Jerome chuckled once more and said, "Ethan, you do more than succeed. As a matter of fact, because we like you so much, we wanted to ask you if you would like to accept that management position".

At this point, Ethan truly felt as though he were dreaming. How could so many things happen inside of his mind in the span of just a few minutes?

One minute he was sure he was about to get fired, lose his job and not have any source of income to pay for necessities such as gas, food, and bills, the next minute he was told *No, you're actually doing a great job and we want to keep you on board*, and then now, finally *Do you want to become a manager and get even more money?*

"Are you serious? I.. uh-" Ethan was visibly shocked and taken aback by the offer which Jerome noticed but didn't mind. In fact, he prodded in to say "I know you weren't expecting the offer right now but I just figured I would throw it out there and see what you think about it. Of course, if you are comfortable with the position you have now and would rather stay here as a sa-"

"No, no, no, I'll-" Ethan was out of breath again. "I'll definitely take the management job. Wow. Seriously, thank you so much. I truly don't know what else to say right now. I'm sorry", Ethan commented. "No need to be sorry, and don't worry - I know you're going to make for one hell of a manager", Jerome replied.

At this, Ethan stood up quickly to shake Jerome's hand - which he noticed was more firm than when he first shook it when he applied to this job - before he finished up the rest of his work duties for the day.

Ethan went home that night and looked happier than he had been in months, because he was, and Kathryn noticed it too, the second he walked through the front door. Not only could she tell from his smiling, but his posture told her all she needed to know.

"Hey, hun! How was work?" she asked happily. She was hoping he was going to answer with a long story instead of just saying "Good" because that answer wasn't going to cut it for her today. She knew that he was happy about something and she wasn't going to rest until she found out what it was.

"Oh, you know, the usual", Ethan answered but as soon as the words spilled out, his slight smile suddenly turned toothy and his eyes quite literally lit up. "Come on, you know it was better than the usual", Kathryn prodded with a smile on her face too.

"Okay, okay, but you're going to want to sit down for this, trust me", Ethan insists. Without any hesitation, his wife walks briskly to the kitchen table, pulls out a chair, and sits down on it. Ethan follows suit and places his hands on the table. He does a slight drum roll without even intending to.

A few seconds go by but Ethan doesn't say anything. He is hoping that Kathryn will ask him once more "What happened? Is there any news?" which is exactly what she says after about five seconds or so.

"Actually yes, there is", Ethan says. "Jerome called me into his office today during the middle of my shift. He says that he and Phillip have been so impressed with my work ethic ever since I started working there that they want me to become a manager now".

At this, Kathryn's eyes nearly brim with joy and her mouth hangs open as she proceeds to jump out of her chair in excitement, all while Isabella sits on the couch watching her favorite television show *The Addams Family*.

"Oh my god, hun! That's amazing!" she expressed. But then she had a worried look on her face momentarily. "Please tell me you said yes. You *did* accept the position didn't you?" she pressed.

"I sure did!" Ethan exclaimed as the two began to embrace one another, with Kathryn planting a small kiss on her husband's forehead which left a red lipstick mark. To Isabella, the only thing in the world that mattered was what was going to happen to Gomez and Morticia Addams, what partner she was going to choose for a class project, and what tee-shirt to put on in the morning.

She knew that her father was searching for a job but even then, her childlike innocence came out on top. In her mind, nothing bad could ever happen to her dad or her entire family for that matter.

However, she did see that her parents were both visibly and audibly *Oh my god hunny, I am so proud of you!* happy and so she was happy in return. As soon as a commercial break was in order, she proceeded to scoot off of the worn brown-faux leather couch and walk up to her mother, asking "What happened?".

"Daddy just got a brand new job, hun! He's going to be a manager at the antique store here!", Kathryn was practically brimming with joy. Isabella didn't exactly know what a managerial job entailed, but she had certainly heard the word before and knew that it was a big deal.

"Yay, Daddy!", Kathryn said enthusiastically which made both of her parents giggle for a few beats. At this moment, the Newton family felt like they were actually a family for the first time in a while. Their lives had been fairly normal for a few months ever since Ethan was working as a sales representative, but they weren't truly happy until today. Ethan hadn't seen Kathryn smile like this in months and it warmed his heart.

Ethan gave Kathryn a big hug while caressing her long blonde hair, gently running his fingers through every strand, while Kathryn was starting to form tears into her eyes. After hugging his wife, Ethan bent down and gave his daughter Isabella another big hug, which sort of took Isabella for a surprise. It was the biggest hug she had ever gotten. At this instant, the Newton's lives were normal. But it wouldn't stay that way forever.

*

Ethan had spent the majority of the next decade of his life wallowing in sorrow and misery. How was it possible that somebody so near and dear to your heart could be taken so soon? Ethan already knew just how fucking irritating cancer was, but it had since grown personal to him.

When he turned sixty, he had taken ownership of the antique store in his home city of Newryst, which turned out to be a much more well-suited job for his age and his hobbies later in life. He enjoyed looking at all the fascinating items customers would bring in. Some items that were brought in were so valuable that Ethan thought it crazy that somebody living in such a strange city as Newryst of all places would own those particular items.

Throughout his tenure at the store, he had seen the strangest things enter the building. One time, somebody had brought in an old, tattered bunny mask that once belonged to one of the members of the city's infamous cult known as The Bunnymen; a large group of individuals who took pride in kidnapping children on or near their birthdays before ultimately killing them in vicious and unthinkable ways.

And even though at this point in time there were rumors of The Bunnymen still around, nobody had seen or heard from them in several years, causing many city residents to suspect that they have gone into hibernation. Maybe their resurgence is just around the corner.

It was items like that which truly fascinated Ethan because of just how rare they were. Even though he hated to admit it, sometimes he genuinely wanted to steal some of the stuff that was brought into the store. He wanted to go right up to one of the display cases and just take it.

Nobody will ever notice, he thought. However, he knew that simply wasn't true. After all, he wasn't the only person working there, and plus, the store was equipped with dozens of security cameras which only makes sense for a horrific city such as Newryst where thieves, creatures, and the unknown stalk unsuspecting prey.

But he found that he really enjoyed his job and actually looked forward to going in every single day. A lot of people his age would be salivating over the mere thought of retirement, but not Ethan. He wanted to retire one day, but he just knew the time wasn't right to do that at the moment.

It was his belief that retirement is something that you can feel deep inside your body almost like true love. You don't need anybody or anything in the whole world to tell you that you're in love. You just know it, balls to bones. The same thing can be said about retirement. When you know it's time to retire, you know.

Perhaps Ethan should have retired earlier after all.

On a snowy day in December, Ethan was just about to close up the store when an elderly gentleman walked in, looking around in a confused state, almost as if he simply wandered inside without even knowing where he was.

Jesus. I hope I'm not like him when I'm even older, Ethan thought. Apprehensively, Ethan asked "S-sir? Can I help you with anything today?".

The old man slowly turned his head toward Ethan with a bemused expression on his face before eventually grinning so wide it looked like it physically hurt his jaw. The smile struck Ethan as a surprising mixture between heartwarming and terrifying.

"Oh! Yes! I'm so sorry, please forgive me", the old man said. "I just have a little something that I wanted to bring in today if that's okay."

"Let's have a look at it", Ethan answered, before the old man slowly extended his arm out toward Ethan, setting down a medium-to-large sized music box on the glass countertop in front of him.

Ethan was visibly perplexed. *Is it just a music box?* "What's the story behind it and how old is it? What makes it special?", Ethan staggered, trying his best to sound authoritative and important.

Ethan was surprised to hear the old man laugh at this as if it was the funniest thing he had ever heard. "You have no idea, do you? This is from the Army Camp that was stationed here in

Newryst. There was a camp here all the way back in the 1900s, but I suppose you must not have been around at the time".

"Somebody had a music box with them at an Army camp?", Ethan asked. "Yes, it supposedly kept all of the men focused and gave them the courage they needed to get through everyday life out in the trenches", the old man answered.

"Alright, well, how much do you want for it?", Ethan questioned before the old man stated that he just wanted twenty dollars for it. *Is this guy out of his mind?* "Twenty dollars? Uh-yeah, sure. I'll ring you up over here", Ethan said before the transaction was complete.

As the old man walked outside the door and into the blistering cold, Ethan yelled back at the man "Stay warm! Be safe out there! It's nasty". The old man simply said, "I hope you stay safe too". But it wasn't until later that Ethan realized the old man wasn't referring to the weather.

When the man left the store, Ethan immediately began inspecting the strange music box that looked as though it were carved from the most precious gems known to mankind. It looked runic and ancient yet crystalline and new at the same time. It was the most beautiful object Ethan had ever laid eyes on.

Ethan started to play the tune which he imagined was probably supposed to be soothing and peaceful, but the song this box played caused goosebumps to break out all over his body. It wasn't like it was terrifying to hear, but it certainly wasn't anything pleasant, either.

The tune continued playing before all of a sudden…

WHAM!

A series of loud banging noises could be heard coming from somewhere inside the store before all of the lights except for a few went dim.

"Hello? Is anybody out there? Show yourself!", Ethan yelled. Sweat instantaneously began to trickle down his cheeks and the back of his neck. Then, nearby, low growling noises were slowly approaching, making their way up to where Ethan was stationed at the front of the store, behind the glass countertop.

Even though he felt like a coward doing it, Ethan simply closed his eyes and put his hands over his head despite knowing it would do jack shit to protect him if there really was some ravenous animal inside the store.

But upon opening his eyes once again, Ethan was stunned to find that the lights in the store were slowly turning back on, one by one. But when he turned his head, he let out a guttural scream after he noticed a group of four skinwalkers slowly stalking toward him.

"What do you want? What the *fuck* are you?!", Ethan screamed. To his surprise, one of the creatures actually answered him.

"We know you live a miserable existence. You have been living in Hell ever since your friend John died", the lead creature said. "We promise that we will bring him back to life for you, with the power of this music box in your hand. All you have to do is allow one of us to play the music box. Then you can see your friend again. It will be like no time has passed since you've last seen him".

"How is that possible? It's just a fucking music box", Ethan replied in a surprisingly steady tone considering the circumstances. "All you have to do is put trust in us", the lead creature said.

At this, Ethan made a quizzical face which the lead creature instantly recognized as apprehension. "I understand how you must be feeling right now. You're probably terrified". *That's an understatement.*

"Just let us play a song with this box, and all will be right. We promise", the lead creature said before beckoning Ethan to hand him the music box to which he eventually obliged. "Thank you", was the creature's only response.

Ethan watched on as the creature wound the box which let out the same unsettling tune that played just moments ago.

But almost immediately, Ethan felt absolutely sick to his stomach. It felt as if his intestines were being wrung out like a sponge, and his stomach lining was being shredded by a chainsaw blade embedded deep inside his body.

Ethan let out the loudest, most painful scream imaginable, taking even himself by surprise. There he lay, writhing on the floor in sheer terror and agony as the group of creatures stood right next to him, continuously winding up the music box while looking down at him.

Slowly, Ethan's soul began to whisk away inside the music box. The soul was visible in the air and shined brighter than any soul the creatures had seen in years. As soon as the music box closed and no sign of Ethan ever having existed, the lead creature smiled before telling his companions "He's pure. He has raw, untamed power that we haven't seen in a human since the Feast of Ravenwood. We can use him later on."

103.9 NEWRYST FM

2034

The city of Newryst has a current population of 683,000 and continues to grow more and more each day. A bustling city full of busy workers and students trying to get to and from college, many residents of Newryst enjoy listening to local radio station 103.9 Newryst FM as a way to keep up to date with important news in the area.

But many listeners tend to tune in simply to listen to the banter between the show's two hosts James Weinberger and Duncan Richardson, who get along perfectly fine when discussing things they agree upon but it's the exact opposite when they disagree.

The following is a transcript from a live recording broadcast to the 103.9 Newryst FM radio station on October 19, 2034.

J: Good morning Newryst residents! You are listening to 103.9 Newryst FM - the city's number one radio show, and your ultimate source for the most up-to-date news going on in the area. I'm your host James Weinberger

D: And I'm your host Duncan Richardson.

J: Today's date is October 19, 2034, which marks just twelve days until Halloween Night, and if the recent pattern of weather here in Newryst is any indication, if you're a parent, you're going to want to make sure that your kids are dressed appropriately for when they head out to do some trick-or-treating.

D: For sure. This has always been sort of a cold city but recently temperatures have been as low as -29 degrees Celcius, which is definitely a bit of shock considering it's only October. We're not used to experiencing this kind of cold until late November at the earliest.

J: Now, there's no snow on the ground as of right now which is good, but folks, don't be surprised if that ends up happening soon because, in Newryst, anything is possible.

D: You're exactly right James. I remember about six years ago, I was driving my son to school for his first day of middle school - this was September 4th, mind you - and we got snowed in like you wouldn't believe. Of course, the show must go on - or in that case, schooling must resume - so I still had to take him to school that day... but yeah... the weather isn't looking too good right now.

J: Wow, that's unbelievable. I honestly remember something like that happening but it definitely doesn't seem like it was six years ago at this point. We're getting old, aren't we Duncan?

D: Don't remind me. I've been living in this city now for about twelve years and even though it's a lot of fun and the people here are all great… more and more each day, I just start to feel like… man I'm getting old. How much time on this planet do I have left? You know? I know I'm only fifty-two, but still. We live in a world where literally anything could happen at any time.

J: I totally get that. But I don't think you have a whole lot to worry about, honestly. As you said, you're only fifty-two years old and you're extremely healthy, you'r-

D: That's true.

J: It is true. I've known you for what feels like my entire life and I've always known you to be the healthiest person I've ever met. Plus, you're also a germophobe so I don't think I've ever seen you get sick even. I mean seriously, the fact that you're never sick kind of makes me want to do that whole "no handshaking" thing that Howie Mandel does.

Duncan laughs, then sighs quietly.

D: I guess you're right about that. But on the other hand, some part of me just keeps thinking about the afterlife… what comes next… all that stuff. You know what I mean? Like… I truly hope there *is* something after we die. To think that we all die and we just live in eternal darkness with absolutely nothing left, no knowledge of anything… it just terrifies me.

J: I'm a firm believer that there is something after we die. The universe as a whole is just so fascinating and there are all these different layers... these... structures to the universe. Do you seriously mean to tell me that humans just live on a little place called Earth, die, and then that's it? Doesn't really sound right to me. But why are we even talking about this in the first place?

D: I don't know. I guess it just slipped into my mind. Once I start to think about things like this, I don't ever really stop until I feel comfortable knowing certain things.

J: I know what you mean, but... don't you think this entire conversation is a little bit too personal for us to be discussing live on the air? I mean, right now, we have over eighty-thousand people listening to this broadcast. Do you really feel comfortable talking about this?

D: Folks; I'm sorry if this conversation is making you a little uncomfortable. I guess it's just... not something that I can control. So if this is getting a little too dark and introspective for you, then please feel free to turn the station off or switch ahead to the next one.

J: I bet that's something you never thought you'd say. Openly inviting our listeners to switch stations!

James and Duncan both laugh.

D: But then I also just start thinking about, if there is an afterlife whether it's heaven or someplace else, it surely *has* to be better than the world that we're currently living in, don't you think so?

J: That's what all those people who were pronounced dead and came back to tell their story always say, at least. People say that you're greeted at the gates of Heaven and you see some sort of flashback to all the most crucial moments of your life.

D: Yeah... I also just hope against everything else, that my daughter is up in Heaven if there is one. I hope she's okay. I just want to be there with her more than anything else. To hug her and tell her that I love her.

Complete silence for ten seconds.

J: Look, I-uh... I'm sure she knew that you loved her more than anything.

D: God, I truly hope so. I think about it every single day. Day and night. I just wish there was some legitimate way to communicate with her and see how she's doing. If there is an afterlife. I don't believe in all that psychic stuff, though.

J: So you're not a fan of *Long Island Medium* I take it?

James laughs

D: Absolutely not! I think all of those mediums are just frauds who are in it to steal people's money. There's some special sort of technique they use that works ninety-nine percent of the time. There's some sort of practice to it. Like, people could write books about the teachings of how to be a medium because that's all it is.

J: There you go! That's a book idea if I've ever heard one! You can call it *The Art of Being a Medium 101: How to Scam People for the Betterment of Yourself.*

James and Duncan both laugh

D: And you know people would actually buy it too! That's the sad part! It would probably wind up on some book website's best-sellers page. Would I be happy? Tough to say. On one hand, I'd be quite rich but on the other hand, I'm selling some phony book. And if-

Duncan stops to glance over at James, who is sitting in his chair, listening intently to something in his earpiece.

D: *mouthing*: What is it? What's going on?

James holds up one finger to indicate Be patient.

J: Alright folks, you know that over at 103.9 Newryst FM we like to joke around a lot and be silly, but I promise you that what I'm about to say next is not any sort of bit we're doing.

Duncan wears a nervous yet interested expression on his face.

D: What's going on?

J: We have just gotten word that there has been some sort of a mutated viral infection outbreak raging throughout the city. As of right now, there are over three hundred people whose life has been taken from them as a result. If you're about to try to exit off the highway right now to leave the city, good luck.

Far off in the distance, a loud booming can be heard piercing the sound barrier in the sky. Upon further inspection, it appears to be...

D: James, we need to get out of here right now! Let's go! Let's go!

James and Duncan both take off their earpiece and flee from the building.

The following is a description of events directly after the taping of the October 19, 2034 episode of 103.9 Newryst FM.

James and Duncan run from the building as fast as they can, weaving their way through the parking lot as a series of massive meteor-shaped objects crash down into the city of Newryst. Far off in the distance, the only sounds that can be heard are those of people screaming and crying, and emergency service sirens blaring rapidly.

The two men are not able to get far. Just as soon as they are about to enter their respective vehicles, another meteor-shaped object plummets down into the parking lot right next to where Duncan stands; the blast radius causes him to go flying backward.

"Duncan! Duncan! Holy shit!" James yells as he rushes over to aid his radio-show co-host and best friend.

"It's okay. I'm okay", Duncan breathes slowly. But it's clear to both of them that it's definitely not okay. The only proof James needs to know that his friend is not going to make it to the next morning is by simply looking at him.

His leg has been blown off from the blast radius, leaving behind a bloody, pulpy stump that appears to have been jaggedly cut with some sort of rotary saw. The shirt that Duncan wears has been completely torn apart, and now, James can see a massive crater-sized hole in the side of Duncan's chest.

"Get out of here. Please", Duncan urges. "You have to get out of here".

"No. No, I can't. I need to help you", James insists. "It's no use, I'm going to die. I have accepted it".

"I know that you're terrified of dying, Duncan. I don't want you to have to go through this alone".

But Duncan's reply genuinely takes James by surprise. "I'm not afraid of dying anymore. I just want to see my daughter again. Now is my chance. Don't take this away from me. I'm begging you".

James can only look on in complete befuddlement as he holds Duncan's dying frame. As he slowly raises his head and looks towards the city skyline, all he can see is the city he loves more than anything else in the whole entire world crumble bit by bit.

Although he can't see any citizens from where he's crouched holding Duncan's lifeless corpse, he knows that it will not be a pretty sight. Second by second, more meteor-shaped objects come flying into the city, creating loud booming noises. The sound of impact resembles that of a nuclear blast.

James realizes now that there is absolutely nothing he can do. He is stuck here, in the real-world equivalent of Hell. As the world crumbles to ash around him, James stands up and says "God help us a-".

HIVES

Anna's life is just like anybody else's who lives in the city of Newryst. She has a typical nine-to-five job working as a bank teller, she goes home every night to her husband of three years named David, and she has two dogs named Taylor and Becky.

And, just like a lot of the city's residents, Anna and David's ideal way to end the night is by throwing on one of their favorite horror movies.

Horror was the one thing that brought them together in the first place. On August 24, 2019, Anna was browsing the local book store as she typically did on Saturday mornings; the only day she would ever go book shopping.

It was one of those strange things that she simply couldn't explain. Sure, the book store was always more crowded on a Saturday because it was the weekend and everybody was off work, but she found that she couldn't enjoy the whole experience on a weekday.

That day it was extremely windy and it rained like a bastard.

It only started raining that morning, meaning that there were hundreds of people walking down the streets dressed in summer clothes such as shorts, fedoras, button-up shirts, and even some flip flops.

Of course, there were some people who had dressed appropriately and anticipated the rain, including Anna, who always made sure to check the weather before going outside anywhere for that very reason.

Anna loved reading books more than anything else in the world. As soon as she moved into her new house, one of the first things she bought for the couch was a throw pillow that read "A house without books is like a body without a soul". But as much as she enjoyed reading, she only ever really read horror novels.

That's not to say she didn't think other novels were good. She had read all of the young adult fantasy series *Throne of Glass* by Sarah J. Maas and had cried by the time she got to the final book. She loved reading *The Giver* by Lois Lowry and *Rebecca* by Daphne du Maurier.

But horror was the one book genre that made her the most comfortable. For some people, horror was terrifying and of course, that made sense. After all, horror novels or movies are supposed to creep you out. And while Anna was creeped out whenever she read horror, she found herself smiling whenever she picked up a new story.

So on that day, she went to the section that she always went to first - horror. She was perusing the area, trying to find a

Stephen King book that she hadn't read yet when a man with short brown hair and a long, dark beard also came into the aisle, seemingly looking in the same area as Anna.

The man cleared his throat. "So... uh... you like Stephen King?", he asked. "Yeah. Yeah, I do", was Anna's reply. "That's nice. Do you have a favorite book?", the man queried.

"Well, I finally managed to finish *It* a month ago and it was probably the one that freaked me out the most. So yeah, probably *It*", Anna responded before finally following up with "How about you? What's your favorite?".

"It's a really good book for sure, but I think I'm more of a *'Salem's Lot* kind of guy myself", the man answered. From that point on, the two spent a solid thirty minutes talking about King and other horror books. About their jobs and hopes for the future.

They went on two dates after that before they soon realized that they were made for each other and immediately began dating.

As with any couple, Anna and David had their problems and their fights, but they always managed to make things work. Even when David was having severe financial problems, Anna stuck around to help out and they never broke up even when they were in danger of losing their home.

So here they were - sitting on the couch browsing various streaming services - when Anna realized "Hey babe, you never saw that new *Pet Sematary* remake did you?" before David answered that he did not.

"Well, is there any reason why?", she pressed. "Not really, I guess I just kind of missed it when it was in the theatre", David responded. The two then agreed to throw it on and they were instantly taken back to their first date when they bonded over all of King's work.

As the couple lay in each other's arms on the couch, Anna began to have a bad itch on her back. At first, she would only itch it every few minutes and David didn't think too much of it.

But when she started to itch ferociously, he eventually asked her what was wrong. "Here, I can pause it for you if you want", David offered, to which Anna said, "Yeah, okay. One sec, I'm just going to the bathroom really quick".

"Babe? Do you need anything at all?", David asked Anna but she had insisted that she would be fine.

As soon as Anna went into the bathroom and closed the door behind her, she noticed that her usually beautiful, smooth skin had now taken on a darker, more sunken-in look. *Well, I was up 'til 2 AM last night*, Anna thought. *It's probably just the lack of sleep kicking in.*

But as each second went by, she looked sicker and sicker. Her skin took on a disgusting yellow-ish color that made her look like she had been infected by some kind of strange virus or disease.

In addition to her rapidly changing skin, Anna's itch on her back grew more and more irritated. She had never had an itch so bad in her entire life. Taking off her shirt, she noticed that her breasts had also begun to sag seemingly out of nowhere.

Just the night before, while changing into her new pair of clothes after showering, her breasts had looked just the same as they always did. But now, they looked like the breasts of an eighty-year-old woman.

Anna realized she should probably feel utterly terrified about her body quite literally changing in front of her very eyes in the reflection of the bathroom mirror, but more than anything else at that moment, the itch was getting on her nerves.

As she reached her hand to her back to scratch, she noticed that her skin felt drastically different. Scaly and rough. Patchy and hive-like. Anna could only stand and stare at herself in the bathroom mirror, constantly scratching her body that was beginning to resemble a humanoid more than an actual, living, breathing human being.

Then, a knocking sound was coming at the door - it was David, wondering what his wife was doing in the bathroom for so long.

"You okay in there?", was David's question. There was a long pause before Anna replied with "No".

David then proceeded to turn the knob on the door, but it was locked. "Honey? Can you open the door? You're worrying me now".

Then, just a second later, Anna had unlocked the door to allow

David to enter. She had prepared for her husband to take one good look at her before vomiting on the floor or perhaps run away screaming, call medical services, or take her to a hospital.

But when David opened the door, Anna was absolutely shocked to find that he was in the exact same condition she was in. His face was a sickening yellow, his eyelids were droopy and his bones were sunken in. His head resembled that of a skull. His brown hair and long beard were still there, but both now took on a scruffy, unkempt look that creeped Anna out.

Anna let out a shrill scream which took even herself by surprise. Why had she not been this terrified when she saw herself look this way? She supposed it was different to see somebody else look that way too. To realize it's not just you, but the love of your life that has been affected by this strange condition.

At this, David took a few steps back. "Wh-what?" he stammered. "What's wrong? Why are you screaming?".

Anna yelled, "Look at you! What happened? Oh my God, David!". She felt like she was getting lightheaded and was seconds away from collapsing on the ground from extreme shock.

David hurriedly entered the bathroom with Anna where he took a good long look at himself in the mirror before wearing a befuddled expression on his otherwise grisly face. "What do you mean?", he breathed. "I look the same as I always do. I got a haircut the other day but you've already seen that", he chuckled briefly before wearing a serious face once more.

Anna only stood and stared at her husband, his skin peeling off slowly. Each second that ticked by, a little bit more of his flesh drooped to the ground in a horrifically gross and foul manner.

"You're telling me you don't see the way you look right now?", Anna asked. David still had a look of complete and utter confusion on his face. Anna realized the only way for him to understand what she was seeing with her own eyes was for her to tell him *exactly* what she was looking at, no matter how crazy he may think she sounds.

"David, your fucking *skin* is peeling off! You look fucking awful! What happened to you? Your flesh is everywhere. You don't see that?".

Now, David looked absolutely horrified but it wasn't because he finally realized what he looked like in Anna's eyes. He was horrified because he thought that his wife had gone totally mad.

He knew that she wasn't joking just by the manner of her voice a moment ago. David could always tell when Anna was being playful with somebody. She had this natural, playful inflection in her voice that would be obvious for even a complete stranger to tell she wasn't being serious.

But the tone of voice that she just used was one that David had recognized. She was telling the wholehearted truth. At least, the truth that she believed.

He slowly made his way toward his wife, creeping up on his tiptoes ever-so-slightly so as not to startle her or make her uncomfortable. Much to his surprise, she willingly embraced him and the two hugged each other for what felt like a year but was, in all actuality, more like a minute or two.

As David began to let go of the embrace, he slowly started to turn into a pile of goop and blood. His entire body faded away into nothing more than a rotting pile of flesh, which, in return, caused Anna to let out the loudest scream she had ever produced in her life.

She collapsed on both knees, clawing her hands through the flesh, some part of her brain hoping that what she was looking at was just some terrible, confusing illusion. But as the seconds passed, she knew that this was no illusion.

She was holding the remains of her beloved husband, who just a few seconds ago, was very much alive and was talking to her, trying to calm her down.

Her tears and her fists pounded the floor in a barrage of fury, paranoia, and disorientation. Out of nowhere, Anna felt her entire body slowly fade away from existence; the feeling she thought an astronaut must feel if they were getting pulled in by a black hole.

She fought harder than she had even thought possible to keep herself alive, but it was no use. First, her legs disintegrated into a pile of rotting flesh on the ground, then her torso, and arms. Although she knew this was the end, she continued to scream while the rest of her body faded into total nothingness.

LAST SHIFT

When sixteen-year-old Joe proceeded to pedal his way down to his best friend Tanner's house on Norberry Lane, he was growing uncomfortable by the lack of noise around him, which only made him ride faster and faster, just so he could see his friend again and finally have somebody to talk to. To finally break this absolutely intolerable silence.

As he pulled into Tanner's driveway, he felt a shiver go up to his spine. He hadn't been here in a little longer than two weeks now (which was a new record for him) and felt like he hardly recognized the place anymore. It looked oddly unfamiliar and almost like a completely different house, but he wasn't sure if it was just because of his absence of being here or something else.

Nevertheless, he propped his bike up against the siding of the house, walked up the steps and pressed the doorbell, and heard Tanner's new dog barking away, enthusiastic about seeing who this new visitor was. After about fifteen seconds, Tanner opened the door and grinned so wide that it surprised even Joe. He had seen Tanner smile many times but he never saw him smile quite like that.

As if on command, following right in Tanner's footsteps was his Boston Terrier named Willow, which ran playfully up to Joe's feet who then proceeded to swoop him up off the ground and pet his head. The canine didn't know if he trusted this strange human yet but eventually looked more soothed and sleepy by the second.

"He's so adorable!" Joe exclaimed. "I know, right!" Tanner excitedly replied. The two continued to look in wonder at the animal as if it were one of the seven wonders of the world before Tanner eventually asked "So... what do you want to do?".

"I was thinking maybe we could head on down to the Blockbuster and see if there are any good movies we can rent", Joe responded. "Sure, that sounds fun", Tanner said with that smile still on his face.

"Hold on, let me just get my bike out of the garage, and then we can head out," Tanner answered. After a few moments, the overhead door opened and the two friends rode out of the neighborhood toward Main Street where their favorite store in the world - Blockbuster Video - was located.

Although Joe and Tanner had never brushed up on the history of the building (after all they didn't have computers in their homes), the Blockbuster Video on Main Street had been constructed eight years ago. It was one of those buildings that the friends had simply assumed was there since the beginning of time. *Oh, the childlike innocence.*

Joe and Tanner absolutely cherished walking inside that store and wafting in the smell of DVD cases, popcorn, candy, and hell even pure excitement. They loved renting out a movie, going home, watching it, and having a blast with it even if the movie wasn't their favorite, but always dreaded having to go back to the door and slide their DVD case through the returns slot.

When they walked in, they both knew that they wanted to rent out a horror film. Their parents would never let them pick a horror film if they were accompanying their children but since their parents were not with them, as far as they were concerned, they could choose any film they wanted.

Immediately their attention was caught by the DVD case of *Troll 2*. "Look at all these weird creatures on the front cover! This will be super creepy". Upon deciding upon the film and taking it up to the front counter, the employee whose name tag read Cassandra, scanned the case and then asked them "So, I take it you guys are fans of the first movie then?".

"Actually no, we've never seen it before. We just thought the cover looked really cool", Joe answered.

"Well, in my opinion, you guys aren't missing much. But I hope you enjoy it". "T-thanks" Joe muttered while Tanner was bobbing up and down on his tiptoes with his hands in his pockets. It was at this moment when Joe realized that they didn't have too much candy to watch the movie with so he picked up a packet of Nerds, two Twix bars, and a bag of M&Ms, to add to the total.

Joe paid in cash, and upon receiving the DVD and candies,

the two kids said their thanks to the cashier and walked out alongside Tanner.

After they left, the store was completely empty. Usually, the Blockbuster was flooded with teens and young adults perusing through the aisles, chatting about school, films, and girls but tonight was different. The air in the video store felt odd and chilly that night, and Cassandra found herself putting her beige button-up sweater over top of her blue and yellow Blockbuster employee uniform.

She became so bored that she ended up reorganizing the membership card stacks, dusting the shelves, and even sweeping the floors. She was at the very back of the store when she heard the doorbell chimes go off. Overjoyed that she finally had a customer to tend to, she promptly made her way back to the counter, waiting for the customer to bring up a movie to rent and ring the individual up.

But there was just one problem - she didn't see anybody in the store. She wasn't going to call out "Hello?" because she thought that maybe the customer was just hard to see because they may have been off in a corner. Three minutes went by and Cassandra still didn't see any customers in sight. She slowly started to feel a terrible feeling rising up within her, festering.

She walked outside of the cashier box and started to roam the aisles, checking to make sure that this customer didn't need help finding something.

Cassandra often hated her job. She hated the minimum wage

pay, hated having to merely stand around for eight hours a day mostly doing nothing but small cleanups such as sweeping the floors and dusting shelves, twiddling her thumbs. She got so bored some days she would call some of her friends from school and talk to them until her manager Thomas would walk in, immediately hanging up just so she wouldn't get yelled at.

And although she despised the job, for the most part, she did enjoy how non-stressful it was and the fact that she *did* get paid. She didn't make much but at least she got *something*. She was happy to simply have a job. Little did she know tonight's shift would be her last.

*

Cassandra didn't really know why she felt so anxious that night. She had been working at Blockbuster for quite a while so she certainly had her fair share of customers who would mosey inside just to take a look, mind their own business, then leave.

But she supposed the fact that her not being able to physically *see* this customer anywhere in the store was what was putting her on edge.

However, she quickly realized that her fears were not unfounded when she began to hear a strange rustling noise accompanied by a voice that sounded pained. She couldn't make out the words but she knew that this voice was saying *something*.

"Hello?", she called out. No answer. "Is anyone in here?", she proceeded to ask but didn't get any response. *Fuck this.* She wished she had one of her co-workers here tonight but her two usual co-workers had both called in sick a few days ago and were still feeling under the weather. It was just Cassandra versus the world.

Finally, Cassandra decided she had better investigate the store just to make sure whoever this person was, wasn't stealing any DVDs. Even if one movie was missing from the shelves, Thomas would notice immediately and he would fire her right on the spot and say something along the lines of "What the fuck happened? Weren't you working that night? How did somebody manage to steal a DVD? You have to open your fucking eyes!".

When she started to slowly stalk her way down the store's various aisles, she felt an extreme nervousness creep up inside her lungs. Each second that ticked by felt like an eternity, and she wished she could simply run out of the store at that very moment and go home. Forget about this stupid job. Her safety was more important.

As she proceeded to walk near the back area of the store, she noticed a large spill of popcorn all over the floor before letting out a loud groan. "Alright, who the fuck spilled this shit all over the god-damned floor?", she asked nobody in particular. She knew that even if there was somebody in the store with her, they weren't going to answer that question and take responsibility.

Cassandra turned and entered the backroom that contained all of the cleaning supplies where she grabbed a broom and dustpan. "Thank fuck tomorrow is my birthday so I don't have to work in this hellhole", she mumbled under her breath as she opened the door that led to the main area of the store.

She began to use the broom to sweep up all the buttery popcorn and all the unpopped kernels into the dustpan when out of nowhere, she felt all of her breath being taken away.

Somebody was suffocating her.

The strange individual was holding up a dishcloth to her mouth where she could taste an unbelievably horrendous and chemical-like substance going inside her body. The more she continued to breathe it in, the more light-headed she felt.

Despite how much she tried to fight back against her tormentor, some part of her brain was telling her to give up and stop fighting back because it was no use. Cassandra was unable to get a look at the person responsible for this incident, but she could tell just by their grip on her that they were outrageously strong. She was just a seventeen-year-old girl that weighed 130 lbs.

Eventually, her entire body went limp and she collapsed on the floor, completely unconscious. The next time she wakes, she will have absolutely no memory of this shift or any of the day's events. All she will know upon waking up is that she is sitting inside a room with dated wallpaper and a strange television directly across from her.

*

Statement from Police Chief Arnold Evans

"It is with great sadness that we confirm that Cassandra Victoria Stevens is missing. She was last seen by her parents before heading out to start her shift at the Blockbuster Video store located at 719 Main Street SW. I spoke to the manager at the store who said he saw Cassandra working her shift that day."

Statement from Thomas Kessler, Manager of Blockbuster Video (719 Main Street SW)

"I saw Ms. Stevens come into work just yesterday evening and she came in with a smile on her face, looking eager to power through the workday. When I saw her there, she was doing a little bit of maintenance - cleaning up shelves, sweeping the floors, and taking calls from a few customers - so I left her to do her own thing. I have always trusted her just like I do my other employees. During her shift yesterday evening, Cassandra was the only person working that evening. Dean (Parker) was supposed to come in but ended up taking a sick day instead, which I was hesitant to give seeing as it how it was the third time that month.

After about twenty minutes of supervising, I proceeded to go into my office where I took a call from the head management team at HQ. I was in there for about thirty minutes and when I came back onto the sales floor, I noticed that Cassandra was gone."

"I started calling her name but I got no response. I picked up the store phone and proceeded to call her home phone number but nobody would pick up. I thought maybe she was just being difficult and decided to leave work extremely early without telling me, or maybe she had just taken a sudden break and she would be back inside shortly, but sadly, I haven't seen her since."

*

Seven days ultimately ended up going by before her parents, Andrea and Scott, were slowly starting to realize that their daughter might be dead. She was never the type of person that would suddenly just vanish. Cassandra, even though she liked to deny it, was the type of person that always spent time with her parents at every opportunity she could. She would go to the grocery store every time with her mom, spend hours outside helping her dad fix various different items like broken stereo parts and a faulty heating part on their 1992 Pontiac Bonneville.

She loved watching sports games with them (especially the Super Bowl). Her mother would always show her how to make various different meals such as fajitas, pesto, soups, and lasagnas.

Cassandra was never the type of person that would up and disappear on her own doing. When she was about six or seven years old, she would throw the occasional temper tantrum and swear up and down to her parents that she was going to run away and that they would never see her again. Of course, her parents knew this wasn't true. They knew that if she even attempted to do something like that, she'd make it down the road five minutes before changing her mind and heading back home.

If things didn't go her way she would scream "I'm running away and you'll never see me again!" and her parents would just say "Okay, sure". They weren't actually encouraging her to go and do it - they knew she would never do something like that - they were simply just too fed up to deal with her behavior. Cassandra, even at a young age, recognized their sarcastic tones of voice which just made her even angrier.

One time she actually did leave the house but only got about two minutes away from her house when a black pickup truck crept down the road and ultimately came to a stop right to the side of Cassandra, who was walking on a sidewalk. "Are you lost, little girl?" the creepy man called out to her.

"No, I'm okay", she responded. She said it nonchalantly but was actually terrified of this man. She didn't have to be old and wise to know that this man was not a friend at all.

"Are you sure? You look like you're lost", the man said. "Come in, I can drive you to my house". Cassandra now didn't know what to say to this stranger. She knew that if continued on with this conversation it was only going to get more terrifying from here. She knew that if she started screaming for help it might agitate the man. She thought he might jump out of his truck, race as fast as he could after her and swoop her up, place her in the backseat of the pickup, and she would never be seen again.

Even though she was only a toddler, she knew that getting in a vehicle with a stranger was the worst possible thing to do. So, instead of answering the man and responding to his comments, she simply stood still for about five seconds while the man watched her with glassy eyes that looked almost bloodshot before she darted back as fast as she could toward her house.

Cassandra was usually quite a good runner in gym class and all of her fellow classmates would talk about how she was as fast as a cheetah, but the speed at which she was running during that moment surprised even herself. She placed one foot in front of the other, one foot in front of the other, one foot in front of the other, barely even paying attention to her surroundings. All she knew was that she had to get out of sight of the creepy man and back to her house immediately.

She started gaining enough speed to the point where she felt confident enough to quickly look behind her just to see if the man in the truck was still nearby, and luckily for her, he wasn't. Even though this definitely made her feel a bit more comfortable, she did not slow down her running speed, just in case the man was hiding somewhere that she couldn't see.

After a solid minute of non-stop running, she got home, opened the front door, and closed it behind her on the way in, her parents asked her "I thought you were running away?". She was too frustrated and upset to even respond, instead, walking somberly up to her room and going to bed for the night.

That was the only time she had ever attempted to do that and her parents knew how much the incident scared her when she told them about it the next day. As a matter of fact, after that day, she had grown a new fear of being kidnapped or murdered in the middle of the night.

Because of these fears, her parents knew that Cassandra would never wander off into the middle of nowhere. As soon as she didn't come home from her shift at Blockbuster, Andrea and Scott both got horrible feelings in the pit of their stomach. It just wasn't like her to not come home and help with dinner. It wasn't like her to not want to watch a movie with them. They waited an hour later than the time she usually came home before they called the store, only to hear from Thomas that he, too, didn't know where she was.

The following day was when they reported her as missing. They both couldn't get any sleep at night, pondering all of the possibilities of what could have happened to their daughter or where she could be at that very moment. The two were naturally prone to worrying and so having their daughter completely gone with nobody knowing where she was made the couple panic like they never had before.

After about two months, however, with not a glimmer of hope in sight, Cassandra's parents simply had to accept the fact that their daughter was more than likely gone for good. They prayed to God that she wasn't dead and that she was simply living in isolation somewhere where nobody else in the world could find her. But even though they were trying to be as hopeful as possible, they knew that was probably silly. Each day, they started to think that maybe their daughter was dead after all. They never would be able to guess that her life had already ended simply because she turned eighteen.

WEBS

Drew was lucky and had a work-from-home job. In the city of Newryst, it could quite literally save your life not having to go into the outside world for even a second. The only problem with the homes in the city? They're mostly all ancient.

Newryst was constructed in 1915 and the vast majority of the houses that were built on the city's foundation still remain to this day. Sure, there's definitely what many folks consider a "rich part" of the city, but obviously, not everyone is able to afford such lavish homes. Most of Newryst's residents have to either settle for a small, decades-old house or pack their bags and look somewhere else.

But Drew was more than happy to purchase this particular house because it had two bedrooms, a nice, spacious living room, a decent-sized kitchen, a basement, and three bathrooms. It definitely has more than what Drew needs seeing as how he lives alone.

Even though he has lived in the house for about eight years now, he still gets the creeps during certain days when he ponders just how old the house he is living in really is. It was one of the homes built in the 1930s, and he could almost swear he heard voices whispering to him while doing his computer work some days.

There he'd sit, typing away, responding to an overwhelming number of emails when he would hear the faintest sound that would jolt him out of his work, no matter how deep he was into everything at the moment. On some days it would just sound like a strange, repeated tapping noise coming from somewhere in the walls, almost like there was a small knock coming on the other side of the wall.

But Drew just assumed it was nothing to worry about. After all, he had been hearing those noises for years and nothing had ever come of them so he figured that if there was something to be worried about, he would've known by now.

However, on some days, he would hear even more unsettling noises; ones that caused him to investigate the entire house even though, every time this happened, he managed to find nothing in the house.

These noises almost sounded like some strange hissing noise. A bizarre gurgling noise. Something being strangled.

One day, Drew was sitting in his office/bedroom, typing away on a document and frequently checking his emails to ensure that his boss wasn't making an effort to contact him. Thanks to modern technology, Drew's boss was able to communicate with the whole team using Discord.

As always, Drew was deep into his work. Many of his friends called him clumsy and a bit of a goofball, but one thing that *everyone* knew about Drew was that, when he starts to focus on something, he truly doesn't break attention until the task at hand is done.

Back when he was in middle school, Drew loved to read more than anything else in the whole world. Some parents would bend over backward to get their children to read even a short, one-hundred-page book, and here was Drew in Grade Six reading six-hundred-page novels and finishing them in just two days.

Usually, he tried not to read anything in class because he knew all too well that it would only spell trouble for him in the long run considering how addicted he was when it came to great novels.

One day while in Mr. Jackie's homeroom class, he busted out his copy of *The Beautiful and Damned* by F. Scott Fitzgerald, a relatively short book in Drew's eyes. He got sucked into the story from the first chapter and refused to put the book down until he got to the halfway point in the book.

As soon as he placed the book down on the desk in front of him, he noticed that every single pair of eyes in the classroom were glued to him including Mr. Jackie, who wore an expression of sheer annoyance and frustration.

So it was no surprise to any of his colleagues when Drew got all of his work done before any of them. Except for this day, where Drew wouldn't be the first to get his work done.

He wouldn't get *any* of it done.

As Drew sat in his desk chair, he started to hear those same clacking noises coming from deep inside the walls somewhere, but because he had heard this sound so many times in his life, he simply stopped for a second to listen closer, then immediately went back to his work.

But the instant he started typing again, the sound could be heard once more. Only this time, it was a bit more aggressive; almost like whatever was making the sound was desperately trying to get somebody's attention.

It certainly had Drew's. Now he stopped completely, listening intently for a good few moments as the sound grew in volume, seemingly getting closer, inch by inch, as the seconds ticked by.

Then, little bits of the wall directly in front of Drew began to crack, causing him to stand up and go to his bed, just so he could distance himself from the wall for the time being. Suddenly…

WHAM!

The wall completely caved outward, and behind it, the world's most massive spider came crawling out of the crack it had made before eventually climbing its way up the wall and ceiling of Drew's office. In the area where the spider came out of, Drew could see what looked to be thousands of webs and nests that had been woven.

It certainly didn't help things that Drew had arachnophobia, either. Upon seeing this gigantic creature, Drew let out the most piercing scream imaginable, which only caused the spider to grow more agitated by the second.

Now, Drew could do nothing but cower in the corner of his room, praying that somehow God would help him out and protect him from this vile insect that was nearly as big as the house itself.

Drew was absolutely horrified by the intensely loud clacking noises of the spider's feet as it moved around on the ceiling. It was so loud that, even if the spider was two rooms away from him, it would sound like it was directly above him.

Please, God, help me. Please. I can't do this. I can't take this. Please.
But God was not listening to Drew's prayers that day. The next thing he knew, he was being picked up by the spider's pincers which only caused him to scream even louder than before.

Because of its intimidating size, the spider's pincers had an unbelievably strong grip. Drew could have been the most muscular guy in the world, and this insect still would've had no problem picking him up like he was nothing but a feather.

Just moments later, Drew was being carried away into the crevasse that the large arachnid had come out of just a few minutes ago, but to Drew, it felt like a year had passed since the spider was in the room.

He let out a series of shrieks but eventually gave up as he realized that there was simply no getting out of this situation, no matter how hard he tried. There was simply no use in trying anymore.

Inside the crevasse was the largest spider nesting area Drew - or anyone in the world, for that matter - had ever seen. There were dozens upon dozens of spider eggs embedded deep into the walls of the interior of the house, as well as several hundred baby spiders that immediately leaped on Drew's skin.

There were so many of them crawling on his body to the point where you couldn't even see a single bare spot. His wails of agony were muffled by the many spiders who had crawled inside his mouth, refusing to get out.

Eventually, the gigantic spider threw him up against a small nesting area, leaving him covered in thousands of webs. Drew had truly never looked worse in his entire life. As he open his eyes, he was absolutely haunted to see tens of thousands of pairs of eyes all trained on him. There must have been hundreds of thousands of pairs of eight-legged freaks surrounding him.

His eyes were so bug-eyed that even Drew himself thought that if they got any larger, they would seriously bulge right out of their sockets. But he just couldn't help himself no matter how hard he tried.

There he lay as prey. Thousands upon thousands of hungry insects looked at him as if he were the biggest and most delicious meal they had ever seen. It would be like if a turkey was still alive before everybody at Thanksgiving dinner dug in - the last thing they would ever see would be pairs of eyes practically salivating over it.

Drew could hear a sickening collective of hisses coming from the mouths of the spiders that were surrounding him. This was it. Without warning, the gigantic spider made one last, long growl before lunging at him, biting off limb after limb until there was nothing left of him except bone for the tiny spiders to chew on as a little snack for later.

WHERE AM I?

My name is Aaron Finlay. I am forty-five years old and I have been living in the city of Newryst ever since I was thirty. Of course, in those fifteen years, I have seen more things here than I care to describe. This place has a reputation for being one of the most fucked up places to live, and that is wholeheartedly true.

If you're a parent and you're reading this - whatever you do - do *not* settle down and have a family in Newryst. It may look like an idyllic city on the surface - there are plenty of schools for kids of various ages to attend, there are dozens of movie theatres, parks, jobs, grocery stores, etc.

Just don't let any of that distract you from the fact that this place is completely and totally fucked. I wish I had come to this realization before it was too late, because now, as I write this letter to whoever reads it one day (*if* anybody reads it), I am confident that I will never see the light of day again.

I think my kidnappers meant to give me a much more powerful drug to knock me out than they did, because I remember everything about what happened a few nights ago. Surely, they didn't intend for me to have these memories still. Right?

It was just like any ordinary day for me. I was sitting at home watching an episode of one of my favorite television shows, unwinding after a hard day at work. I'm a construction worker, currently working on the new Gaffenstein Tower on Main Street. Or, I guess I should say I *was* working on the Gaffenstein Tower because I'm not going to be doing any sort of job anymore.

The night went just as I had planned. I had made my favorite dinner that night - Mongolian Beef. I had my glass of red wine, my feet were kicked up in the air, and my surround sound speakers were turned on. What more could you ask for in life?

Then, I heard the loudest thud imaginable come from directly behind me. It sounded like it had come from behind my front door, but when I quickly spun my head around to see what happened, nothing was there. Of course, I'm not a total idiot. I didn't want to just sit there and pretend like nothing happened so I stood up and walked over to the door and looked through the peephole.

Nothing. The front porch was completely barren and I couldn't even see anybody walking by on the sidewalk. There were zero vehicles driving by in the neighborhood. The only cars in sight had already been parked there hours ago by the neighborhood residents.

I'm kind of paranoid when it comes to loud noises like this. It all started back when I was about nine years old and my parents left me home alone because they were having a date night out and they didn't want me to come with them for obvious reasons. They couldn't find any babysitter on such short notice, but I didn't mind. After all, what kind of a kid isn't excited about the prospect of being left home alone?

It didn't take me long at all to realize that maybe being alone in the middle of the night wasn't such a fun thing after all. I was in my room trying to relax and play with a few of my action figures but I kept getting scared at the faintest noises.

The bathtub in our house had a leaky faucet that would drip or creak every so often. I knew that even at the time, but when I heard it creak that night, it didn't stop me from freaking out, thinking that somebody had broken into our home all while my parents were gone. I had nobody to protect me.

As soon as I started to hear these faint noises, I had wished that my parents would come back. Maybe they would just go on a short date and would be home in an hour or so. They didn't get home for another three hours after I heard that first noise.

And of course, back then there was no such thing as cell phones so it wasn't like I could just ring up my parents' cell phones and tell them I was scared. Even if cell phones were around, it's not like little eight-year-old me would've had one anyway. So I was fucked. It was just me versus whatever sounds I was hearing.

Even though now I'm forty-five, I still get paranoid when I hear noises no matter how quiet or loud they are. But seeing as how I couldn't notice anything unusual on the streets, I figured I would just go back to my couch and continue watching my television program.

A good ten minutes or so went by and everything was perfect. I knew the sound couldn't have been in my imagination, but it kept bugging me. What was that noise? Why was it so loud? But after those ten minutes were up, I suddenly felt an incredibly sharp prick pierce my neck, which caused me to let out a loud groan, causing me to keel forward, gripping my stomach tight.

I felt dizzy almost immediately. My whole head felt as if it were spinning before I ultimately passed out. This was a few days ago. Or, at least I think it was because down here, I really don't have any sense of time or the weather.

For all I know, I could have been down here already for a full year and the drug I was given had knocked me on my ass for months or years. It's hard to say. All I know is that I'm in an incredibly cold and unbearably uncomfortable area. It's dark and gray down here, and I can only see a few feet in front of me.

I have only ever seen my captor once and they look to be a tall, gangly entity with no discernible facial features, and their skin is completely gray. I know that whatever this thing is, it's not human. As for what it is exactly, I have no idea.

But what terrifies me just as much is the fact that I am here with dozens of other people who cannot move or talk. They must have been given the proper drug because I can still move and I can still talk. I just don't do any of those things unless necessary, for fear of my own life.

Whatever that thing is, I don't want it to see me moving around because what if it injects me with a second drug to ensure that this time, I don't move or talk ever again?

To tell you the truth, I don't have any idea why I'm even writing this letter in the first place because I know deep down inside that I'm never going to make it out of here alive. It feels like I've been transported into another universe. Wherever this is, it's nowhere in Newryst unless the city has harbored some horrifying underground facility I've never heard of before.

I guess the reason why I'm writing this letter is for two reasons: one, to help me feel better about the situation I'm in. Of course, I'm absolutely terrified here and I have no way of getting out, so I will never be truly comfortable again. But I find that writing this letter has lifted a weight off my shoulders in a way.

The second reason: to warn anybody who *does* read this letter. *If* anybody reads this letter. If you somehow managed to get a hold of this, please listen to me: Get out of Newryst. Right. Fucking. Now. This city is not at all what it seems. It only continues to grow like a plague each and every day, and I fear for everybody who is currently living there.

I don't care what kind of fancy job you have. I don't care if you've paid off a house in Newryst and have settled down. Get out. Because if they can find me in the comfort of my own home, I promise that they *will* find you.

STORY NOTES

While You Sleep

Man, this one was just weird.

Sleep paralysis has always been something I've been morbidly fascinated by. I've also always thought that there should definitely be a horror movie centered all around the creepy phenomena, but to date, there doesn't exist one and I have no idea why. The mere idea of not being able to move or talk all while a terrifying demon is perched on top of you is absolutely bone-chilling for me.

Gratefully, I have never had to experience sleep paralysis and I pray that it remains that way for the rest of my life. However, I have had to endure an entire year of insomnia which was easily the worst year of my life.

I wanted to inject that bit of my life into the character of Everett, because I know all too well what it's like to lay in bed for hours at a time, not being able to simply shut your brain off and tell it to go to sleep. If only it were that easy, am I right?

But more than anything, with *While You Sleep*, I wanted to make this story one that would be so unsettling for readers to experience that it causes them to be a little bit weary when they go to bed at night. In my opinion, the best possible way to read this story would be to read it in your bedroom alone at night, with just an overhead lamp on.

To tell you the truth, this was the story that freaked *me* out the most personally and the one that gave me goosebumps while writing. Anybody that's ever had insomnia before will tell you straight up that it's one of the worst feelings in the world. Why? Because it is.

As humans, we all know that we have to sleep in order for our brains to be fully functional by the time the morning comes. Even just one night of no sleep will seriously mess you up for the entirety of the next day. The more sleepless nights you have, the more you will start to feel like you're slipping away from reality.

Terrifying hallucinations will start to occur within your world. Sleep deprivation can lead to poor cognitive function, increased inflammation, and reduced immune function. On top of all of that lovely stuff, the longer you go without sleeping, the more your risk for chronic disease increases.

But obviously, falling asleep isn't always as simple as laying in bed and closing your eyes. Those who suffer from insomnia quite literally suffer. You'll be laying there with endless thoughts trailing through your head, just praying that your brain will eventually shut off, but that's sadly not the case for so many people.

I always thought it would be an absolute blast to create a story related to sleep in some way because the lack of sleep is genuinely more terrifying than some monster stories, in my personal opinion. For this story, I wanted to explore a man who would literally rather be a demon serving the Devil in the deepest depths of Hell than have to go through sleep deprivation.

Because he is now in Hell, he no longer has to worry about sleep anymore because, well, he's in Hell. Sleep doesn't exist there, which is the only thing that really matters to him. Sure, he may be a demon but at least he can stay awake for all eternity.

If this story was able to make you even remotely freaked out, then I have accomplished my goal. This story is also the one that I genuinely want to turn into a fully-fledged novel of its own one day. I guess only time will tell if people like you enjoyed this story and want to dive even deeper into Everett's twisted world.

Birthday Bumps

This story was one that I have wanted to tell for a long time but I just didn't know what outlet to use. I initially thought it could make for an interesting short film for years, but I ultimately decided it would fit very nicely in this book of twisted tales.

As you can probably tell, this is perhaps the most sinister and gruesome story in the book. For the majority of the stories in this novel, I wanted to write about some truly strange and unsettling stories involving terrifying entities and demonic creatures while also making it feel relatively grounded. When setting out to write this book, I knew I should probably have at least one or two stories that were grotesque and intensely bloody because when some people think of the horror genre, that's what they think about. I wanted this book to have a little bit of something for everyone.

But, nevertheless, "Birthday Bumps" is a story that focuses less on supernatural oddities and instead, puts its attention on being vile and disgusting. How did I come up with this story, you ask? Well, I was browsing the internet (Reddit, particularly), looking for creepy and off-putting images when I stumbled across a photo of a retro television set stationed inside an empty room that looked like it was taken in the 1980s.

As soon as I saw this, my mind began to churn and I came up with the story of "Birthday Bumps", one of the stories I am most proud of to this day. You also probably noticed that The Bunnymen cult from this story is also mentioned in my story "The Antique Store" as well as "Last Shift". In case you're wondering if this strange cult is going to be in any of my future novels… the answer is yes. But only if there is demand for it. Time will tell.

He'll Be Back

This was the first story I ended up writing for this novel, and it was one that was a little bit difficult to write. Not because I was struggling to come up with a good story idea, but rather, because nearly every word of the story legitimately happened to me and my best friend when we were ten years old.

Yes, really.

My friend was sleeping over at my house that night and, just like we always did, we tried to pull an all-nighter. However, we eventually noticed some objects in my backyard were moving around the area whenever we weren't looking. And, yes, we really did see *something* moving in the shed. My friend also did end up checking the shed later on but was unable to find anything.

To this day, the both of us have absolutely no idea who or what was in the shed late at night, and I don't think we will ever want to know the truth. The one percent of the story that was fake was that we were playing a game called *Merrytown Legends*. There is no such game. That, and my name is not Calvin. Everything else? One-hundred-percent real.

And in case you are wondering, this did indeed happen in 2010, and nothing has ever come of this incident since so I'm assuming that whoever was in the shed that night has no plans of coming back, but it is definitely still something I think about quite often.

My friend and I have had hundreds of sleepovers throughout our childhood, and all of them were great… except for that one. We didn't get any sleep that night, and seeing as how we were ten years old, can you really blame us? Heck, if this happened to me *today* I wouldn't be able to get to sleep that night. This story will forever go down in my history books as one of the weirdest things that has ever happened to me.

The Face

Sometimes all it takes for inspiration to strike me is simply looking at an image on Pinterest or Reddit that startles me and gets my brain churning various ideas of what the picture could mean.

While I was coming up with story ideas for this book, I remember browsing some of the horror communities on Pinterest where I ultimately found an artistic rendering of some sort of unsettling, featureless face. But even though this face didn't have any discernible features, it didn't stop me from getting goosebumps immediately after looking at it, so I just knew that I had to make up a story relating to this image.

I've always wanted to create a short horror story that kind of gets flipped on its head right at the last possible moment. A story that quite literally forces you to re-read the story again just so it becomes even more impactful the second time around.

With *The Face*, I wanted to tell the story of a seemingly normal, innocent young girl who is living alone in the Big Apple with some hopes and dreams. However, she continuously gets bogged down with sleepless nights and extremely terrifying hallucinations of the faceless man.

It's a story that I hope left you feeling uncomfortable while reading it, and it's one that I hope left you more than a little surprised with the last two sentences.

The Antique Store

Alright, so you probably noticed that "The Antique Store" was the longest chapter in this book by a long shot. Technically speaking, this story is so long that it could've been released as a "novelette", but I found that this collection was a better fit for it in the grand scheme of things, and not just because it takes place in the city of Newryst.

I came up with this story over a year ago at this point. I knew I wanted to tell it but I just didn't know how or where it was going to come to fruition. I wanted to make this a story of a man who has an ordinary life with a family. He goes to work every day and has a best friend and the two are inseparable. But as is often the case in our world, life can be a bitch. Cancer strikes and ultimately kills his friend.

He then lives out the rest of his days working because he wants to keep his mind busy. Having him stay at home all day every day with his thoughts is a bad idea and even *he* knows that. And, as you saw in the story, things only get worse from there as a creepy and suspicious elderly man brings a music box to the antique store our protagonist is working at. But it's not just any music box.

It's a music box that summons demons.

But Ethan's life is miserable. Even though it's been more than a decade since the passing of his friend John, life has not gotten any easier. He just wants to see him again. So when one of the demons makes a promise to Ethan that he can see his best friend again, he's more than happy to take that chance, but it ends up costing him his soul. *Literally*.

As for the Feast of Ravenwood, I definitely will be exploring that storyline more in the future… if there is demand. Stay tuned!

103.9 Newryst FM

There's just something so incredibly fascinating about radio broadcasts - at least to me. From the very first day I started writing this book, I knew that I wanted to come up with *some* sort of story relating to an ordinary radio show that people in Newryst frequently listen to. Everything is fine until disaster strikes.

Literally.

Originally, I was going to write this story and have one of the two hosts try to kill each other while broadcasting live on the air, but I didn't really think that made a whole lot of sense, so I went with down the disaster/apocalypse route.

As I am sure you noticed with this chapter, there are definitely a lot of unanswered questions, and the way the chapter ends leaves things open-ended. We don't know what in the world managed to claim James and Duncan's lives other than a strange meteor-shaped object.

This storyline is definitely something I plan to explore in a future book if the opportunity arises, and of course, if there is a high demand in me even venturing back to that specific point of time in the history of Newryst.

Hives

Gross-out horror is one of my favorite story types the genre has to offer. There's just something so morbidly fascinating about somebody who has some strange creature growing on their body. Or in the case of my story, a strange hive-like outbreak growing on an unsuspecting woman's body that she constantly itches, turning her entire body to a pile of rotting flesh.

This is perhaps the story that will be the most bizarre to readers. It starts off simple enough as we follow this young woman and her husband who have a happy life together, but things start to escalate quickly as soon as the woman notices that she is getting very, very itchy...

A lot of the stories in this novel end tragically as you could probably tell by reading them. It never ends with everybody surviving. Or if they do, *something* terrible happens to them, as you saw in "The Antique Store". I wanted to make this story's ending feel hopeless for the main characters. They both embrace each other while they turn to nothing but bones and flesh and there is *no* happy ending to be found for either of them.

Last Shift

Ah, the good old days when Blockbuster Video was still a thing. As a young kid, there were two places that I considered home: my actual house where myself and my parents resided and Blockbuster Video.

Back when I was nine all the way until I was about thirteen, I went on weekly to bi-weekly trips to the local Blockbuster which was gratefully just a five-minute drive from my house. As a kid, my parents would drive me down there so I could look at all the various video games they had to rent for Xbox 360 and PS3 while my parents would peruse the DVD section.

We would have a weekend movie night at my house every other week and the vast majority of the films we watched came from Blockbuster. The first time I ever remember watching a horror movie was *The Hills Have Eyes* on DVD which we ended up renting from our local Blockbuster.

If you were to gather three-hundred film fans and ask them if they miss Blockbuster, I'm willing to bet that nearly every one of them would say "yes". Sure, streaming is great. It's amazing that we live in a world where we can quite literally watch movies with the click of a button, but there was just something so indescribably special about walking or driving down to your local Blockbuster and spending a good thirty to forty-five minutes walking around, taking everything in.

Not only did they have an amazing movie selection, but they had video games and candy and popcorn. Plus, the store smelled absolutely amazing. Seriously, do any of you remember how *heavenly* it smelled in there?

The only thing that sucked about the Blockbuster experience was having to return the DVD or video game at the end of the week by dropping it into the returns slot. I remember legitimately shedding tears when the Blockbuster in my city closed down at the age of twelve. It was heartbreaking to see a piece of my childhood disappear.

Long story short - Blockbuster Video is beloved by millions of people all around the world. There are even documentaries about the company and why it was so amazing. That's why I figured it would be an absolute blast to write a short horror story set inside one of the most beloved places in the world. This was easily one of the most fun stories to write. Now, if you'll excuse me, I think I'm going to dig up my old membership card and cry for a little bit.

Webs

I kind of surprised myself with this story because I genuinely didn't think I had it in me to write a short horror story about spiders, mainly because the biggest phobia I have is arachnophobia. Seriously, I cannot even look at a picture of a baby spider without my entire body wincing. I'm not kidding.

Gratefully, I've never seen anything as big as a tarantula in person before, but if I ever do, I'd probably just scream bloody murder just like Drew did in this story. But you're probably wondering "Why *did* you decide you wanted to write a story about a gigantic spider coming to eat an unsuspecting man?". That's a good question.

I am a massive vintage horror paperback collector and I have a whole ton of books relating to gigantic, evil spiders believe it or not. Have I ever read any of these books? No, and I probably won't ever read any of them in case I read one and feel physically sick to my stomach.

So, really, I know exactly how terrifying spider stories can be. There is just something so inexplicably terrifying about the eight-legged creature and I know that there are millions of people all around the world who share that same fear of spiders as I do, which is why I wanted to share this story.

If you have been reading the story notes for every single chapter so far, you probably noticed how I want to make follow-ups to a lot of the stories I've written for this book. "Webs" is one of the only ones where I simply do not want to. I can't imagine writing an entire novel about spiders since I had a heck of a hard time writing a short one. Now, if you'll excuse me, I think I'm going to take ten showers now.

Where Am I?

This was the second chapter of this book that was written from the first-person point of view, which was certainly fun to write in. Nearly every other story in this book is from the third-person perspective, telling the tales of individuals who were unlucky enough to live in the absolutely terrifying city of Newryst.

With "Where Am I?", I wanted to tell a story written by a man who has lived in this fictitious city for many years and was blinded by the city's horrific history. By the time he realizes that it's not a safe place to live, it is simply too late and there is no chance of him seeing the light of day ever again after having been kidnapped by some sort of unknown, other-worldly entity who brings him to an undesignated location where he will ultimately die.

Although our lead protagonist Aaron knows that he is never going to see the light of day again, he writes this letter in the hopes of it *somehow* finding its way to the public, telling any and all Newryst residents to pack their things and move someplace else because if something terrifying can happen to him, it can happen to absolutely anybody.

ACKNOWLEDGEMENTS

It still feels unbelievably surreal to be sitting here typing out this closing chapter because, long story short, I truly never thought I would ever be able to have the opportunity to have my very own book released. It's one of those things that every writer wants to be able to do, but it doesn't always come to fruition. Writing this out, I feel unbelievably lucky in every way.

It's funny, because all throughout my days at elementary, middle, and high school, I was never the biggest reader. In fact, whenever one of my teachers would pull out a brand new book and announce that we were going to be reading it and analyzing the story and characters, I let out a sigh of defeat. These books never piqued my interest much.

But one day I remember picking up a copy of *The Hobbit* by J.R.R. Tolkien and falling absolutely in love with it, which caused me to reflect and ponder the question "Do I actually dislike reading?". The answer was one-hundred-percent no. All I had to do was find the stories that I genuinely wanted to read. I had to fall in love with characters I was more than willing to fall in love with.

ACKNOWLEDGEMENTS

These days, reading is an essential part of my life and I typically read about eighty books in any given calendar year. There's just something special about holding a brand new book in my hands that I've never read before, eager to dive right in and be whisked away into the author's world.

From the bottom of my heart, I sincerely hope that you were able to be whisked away to my world when reading this book. The stories you have just read were painstakingly hard to write, but the feeling I got most of all whenever I wrote them was satisfaction. Some of the stories in this book have been in my mind for years, desperately clawing for a way out.

My friends will tell you firsthand that I'm always coming up with crazy ideas for various books. I'm always crafting new, bizarre stories in my head that my friends and family are probably sick of hearing by now, so I want to say a heartfelt thank you to everybody who's been by my side throughout this crazy thing known as life.

Nicholas Favel and Tanner Johnson - you had to spend countless years of your life listening to me gush about Taylor and her music on an almost daily basis and yet, somehow, you put up with it. So thank you both for being great listeners and some of my biggest supporters. I'm also glad you were willing to listen to me basically act as a Taylor Swift dictionary every day. And to Matt Knee, Jacob Cucksey, Kyle Van Aswegen - thank you.

Another huge thank you goes to my brothers Austin and Jeremy for being the best brothers a kid could ask for. That, and for listening to me talk about Taylor Swift endlessly as well, of course.

Huge thank you to Ms. Frankemolle and Mr. Walton for being two awesome teachers that helped make elementary school so memorable and fun. Ms. Lowry, Ms. Fong, Ms. Turner, and Mr. Acierto - thank all four of you for being some of the funniest, most encouraging teachers in the entire world.

To Mr. Massey, Mr. Nisbett, Mr. Dumont, Mr. Sorathia, Mr. Roberts, Ms. Johnston, Ms. Kuntz, and Ms. Cunningham for always being some of the best and most helpful teachers all throughout high school. Without all of you, I know for a fact that I wouldn't be the same person I am today. Thank you for all that you did for me and all that you continue to do as teachers.

Whenever I set my heart on writing this book, I wanted to have an old 80s paperback aesthetic to it from the writing style, all the way down to the cover design. In my opinion, a bad book cover can be extremely detrimental to any author because, after all, an eye-catching cover is what grabs people's attention first and foremost when browsing for books online.

So I want to say a huge thank you to my friend Donnie Goodman for designing the absolutely stunning cover of this book. Words cannot even begin to describe how much I love this cover. Donnie - you more than understood the assignment. You went above and beyond and delivered the best possible book cover art I could have imagined in my wildest dreams. The first time I saw the cover, I actually think my jaw might have been on the floor.

ACKNOWLEDGEMENTS

Thank you to one of my biggest writing inspirations Cameron Chaney - without you, I have no idea if this book would even exist, to be honest. After watching his videos for years and seeing him write his own book, I realized "Hey! I can do that too!", so I went ahead and did exactly that. Mr. Chaney, if you're reading this - thank you. I sincerely hope that even just one of these stories was able to give you the creeps or remind you why you love reading. Keep on being you!

Of course, I also want to thank my parents - aka the best parents in the whole entire world. I know that every kid says "My mom and dad are the best in the world!", but I genuinely mean it. You've both been one-thousand percent supportive of me ever since day one. I love you, Mom and Dad.

To my aunts and uncles, cousins, and other close relatives - thank you so much for being highly supportive of me and what I love to do. I'll never understand how I got to be so lucky and have the most supportive family out there, but I am beyond proud to say that I most definitely do.

And to Korynn. It is not hyperbole when I say that without Taylor Swift, I never would have met the love of my life and the girl of my dreams. To make matters short, we both had fan accounts on Instagram where we both started direct messaging each other.

We did this for quite some time and it was only after several months that we proceeded to ask each other where exactly in Canada we were from. To our bewilderment (and extreme excitement) we both said that we lived in the relatively small city of Airdrie which seemed too good to be true. Several dates later, Korynn asked me to be her boyfriend which is the best question I've ever been asked to this day.

Of course, I said yes - how could I not? Korynn, you are the one girl I want to be with forever and evermore. You are the best thing that's ever been mine, and without you, I legitimately have no idea where I would be today.

And of course, thank *you* for reading this book of mine that I poured every little bit of my heart and soul into. I have been wanting to write a horror novel for years and I just didn't know how to go about it. I also didn't know if anybody would even be interested in reading my stories.

But if you have made it this far in the book, then I think it is safe to assume that you managed to read this entire book. If you have, thank you. And even if you didn't read the entire book - maybe it just wasn't for you or up to your standards - I still want to think you for being even remotely interested in this collection.

I know it may sound funny simply because this book is so new at the time of writing this closing piece, but I already have dozens of story ideas for another book that I definitely do want to write if there is demand for it. There are some stories that I've conjured up in my mind that I think are genuinely wild and I hope I get the chance to write about them some day soon.

How can you let me know if you want a second book? It's simple - let me know with some reviews on Goodreads, Amazon, or anywhere else you can review books. It's really the only way that I'll be able to tell there is demand for another book set inside the fictional city of Newryst.

But until then, thank you all so much. For everything.

-Caillou Pettis
January 19, 2022

ABOUT THE AUTHOR

Caillou Pettis is a professional film critic and journalist, writing in the entertainment industry for over seven years professionally. Throughout the years, he has written articles for publications including Exclaim!, Awards Radar, TILT Magazine, Flickering Myth, BRWC, Starburst Magazine, Punch Drunk Critics, Mediaversity Reviews, Vinyl Chapters, Northern Transmissions, We Got This Covered, Screen Rant, The Line of Best Fit, and Beats Per Minute. He has also worked with YouTube channels boasting more than 10 million subscribers and more than 1 billion video views.

He is also a Rotten Tomatoes critic and a member of the TimesUpCritical Film Critics Society, Celebrity Film Awards (CFA), and the Online Film and Television Association (OFTA).

Printed in Great Britain
by Amazon